THE ANALYST

Unsung Hero

Manu. D

First published in 2020 by
BecomeShakespeare.com

One Point Six Technologies Pvt Ltd,
123, Building J2, Shram Seva Premises,
Wadala Truck Terminus,
Wadala (E), Mumbai - 400037
T:+91 8080226699

ISBN: 978-93-90463-03-9

DEDICATION

SatyamThis story is dedicated to all those,

Who fights for the country

Who fights for the loved once

Fights for Family,

To my Parents, and who helped me to write this book is none other than my brother and sister Megha and my Uncle Veeresh Meti.

It is dedicated to the Real Heroes of Country,

Our Indian Army

ABOUT THE AUTHOR

Sangameshgouda D Patil born on 15th August 1995 and he is from Karnataka, is pursuing B.E Engineering. Sangamesh is passionate about creating something in the Technology. And he also pursuing a Android Development Course.

A sci-fi buff since childhood, and he like to watch Sci-fi and Spy movies and read books. Because, of his passion towards the books related to spy THE ANALYST – UNSUNG HERO is born. This is his debut book, and it is the combination of the Emotion and Action. And character is inspired by the Tom Clancy's character called Jack Ryan. He plans to turn this book into Spy – Series.

DEDICATION

SatyamThis story is dedicated to all those,

Who fights for the country

Who fights for the loved once

Fights for Family,

To my Parents, and who helped me to write this book is none other than my brother and sister Megha and my Uncle Veeresh Meti.

It is dedicated to the Real Heroes of Country,

Our Indian Army

ABOUT THE AUTHOR

Sangameshgouda D Patil born on 15th August 1995 and he is from Karnataka, is pursuing B.E Engineering. Sangamesh is passionate about creating something in the Technology. And he also pursuing a Android Development Course.

A sci-fi buff since childhood, and he like to watch Sci-fi and Spy movies and read books. Because, of his passion towards the books related to spy THE ANALYST – UNSUNG HERO is born. This is his debut book, and it is the combination of the Emotion and Action. And character is inspired by the Tom Clancy's character called Jack Ryan. He plans to turn this book into Spy – Series.

TABLE OF CONTENTS

Chapter 1
BEGINNING OF GENOCIDE

13 August 2000

Aleppo, Syria, Unknown Location

A dozen of cars and trucks packed with goods were being transported from Pakistan to Aleppo city. The people involved and their motives remained unknown to the natives of Aleppo city. All of their cars and trucks have been stopped at the centre of the market place.

All of these goods were transported to the old, unused factory for their work. Suddenly family happened to pass by them. One of the family members was a young boy whose eyes caught the sight of the guns and other weapons. Mistaking them as toys, he got interested in them and ran towards the place and entered the factory. As soon as he entered, he saw so many guns and other stuff. He liked all of them; he took one of them and began to leave the factory to show it to his parents. But, suddenly something else caught his attention. He saw tubes with some kind of liquid and stared at them surprisingly. Perhaps they were some kind of cold drinks so; he grabbed one of the tubes and took the gun as well. Just when he was about to leave, a man with gun saw him and yelled at a high-pitched voice,

"Hey boy ! What are you doing? Keep them here and go outside,"

The Boy got afraid and started to run towards his parents when a man started to run behind him to take back the stuffs that belonged to them. Only he knew what they really were.

By then the boy had already slipped out of the factory. Meanwhile, the boy's parents were getting worried because they thought that their son was lost in crowd. So, they started to cry out his name louder, "Asif! Asif! Where are you?"

After getting out of the factory, the boy looked around for his parents but couldn't spot them. So, he began to cry loudly, "Abbu, ammi, where are you? I can't see you, abbu, and ammi!"

On hearing their son's voice, the parents started to run towards the voice that very second. Finally, they got their boy and asked him, "Where were you? We were so scared thinking that we had lost you!"

"Ammi, I got a toy and cold drink for sister!" he produced the things before them.

"Oh, boy! Where did you get them? Whom do they belong to?"

After frantically searching for the boy, the man finally spotted him, but with his parents. He got scared and immediately ran towards the factory.

The boy's father took the gun in his hand and examined it. What he saw shocked him because it was a real gun in the market. A policeman, who was nearby, noticed the father with a gun and ran towards to him and said alarmingly,

"Hey! Put the weapon down otherwise we will shoot you"

His wife, terrified, requested, "No, no it is a mistake, officer! This isn't what you think it is … Please don't shoot!"

People around got terrified and began to run after hearing the policeman's threat. Meanwhile, during this mayhem the boy accidently got pushed into the crowd. The boy's father tried to put the gun down. However, amidst the commotion, the officers thought that the man was attempting to fire the gun. Before the officers could do anything, a massive blast blew up that area, causing the death of 300 people. And after that, people of that city were scared of that blast and the local authorities told the media, "It was accident from the old factory some malfunction of machines that caused the blast"

Same Day

Delhi, India,

RAW Headquarters

Army General Srivastav got information about blast that happened in Syria. After a few days, the army general got a tip from his agent who was working undercover for some years in Syria. So, the general immediately contacted the undercover agent named Uday, functioning under the code name Shabaz.

'So, Uday, tell me you have 60 seconds—what is your tip from Syria? And what is the news about blast?" the General enquired.

"Sir, it is not what you think it is. The blast was not an accident, sir. The local authorities are telling the people what they want to hear sir—"But suddenly the call got disconnected.

"Uday? Hello, Uday?"

Assuming that something has happened to Uday somebody has come to know about him, the General started to delete all the files under the name Uday so that nobody could trace him. If anybody gets a hang of it, it will be danger to the country.

Srivastav considered talking to the prime minister about this situation. He made the call to the prime minister's personal assistant Tiwari to request a meeting with the PM.

"What is it, General? What can I do for you?" the personal assistant, Mr Tiwari, asked.

"It is very urgent to talk to the PM Devansh Singh sir. I want you to arrange a meeting with him today, as soon as possible. It is about our country and some conflict involved," said Srivastav.

Mr Tiwari finally agreed to fix a meeting with PM, and asked the General to come right then. The general immediately left the base to meet the prime minister.

Delhi

PM Office

After about an hour, General Srivastav arrived at PM's office. Mr Tiwari went to inform the PM,

"Sir, General is here to see you, as he had previously informed."

"Okay, then let him in."

Having the affirmation, Tiwari went to the waiting room and said, "General, our PM is ready for you; you may go now."

"Oh, thank you, Tiwari ji!"Srivastav swiftly walked into the PM's room,

"What is it general? What is so important that you want to meet me with such urgency? Is there any problem?"

Yes, sir we got a problem."

What is it? Anything major?" " The PM looked alarmed.

"What do you think, sir? What might it be?"

"Come on, go on … tell me!" PM replied impatiently.

"Sir, did you hear about blast that happened in Syria today?"

"Yes, I heard about that—it was an accident."

"No, sir it wasn't accident," General Srivastav replied.

"What are you saying? How do you know, General?" the PM enquired in shock.

"One of our agents has been undercover in Syria for three years. About an hour ago, he contacted me and told that something is wrong and that the local authorities are hiding something. Sir, he strongly believes that the blast wasn't an accident."

"What's the fix? Does this pose any problem for our country?" the PM asked.

"I don't know sir, While I was talking to my agent, the call was disconnected abruptly.We are guessing that our agent might be exposed, Sir. And as he has tried to contact me, we can rightly assume, something must have gone wrong, Sir!" Srivastav explained.

"Do whatever you have to do to keep our country safe," PM replied.

"Sure, I will keep our country safe, trust me. I will do whatever it takes to ensure that."

Then he left the office and contacted the bureau, "Activate the second software in Syria."

The General's instructions were soon followed. The second software got activated in Syria.

Aleppo, Syria

Unallocated area

As Uday was talking with his chief, he noticed that someone was watching them. He got nervous and looked around, searching for the onlooker but he couldn't focus on any particular face because of the crowd. However, certain on being spied on, he disconnected the call and took a lane. After walking some distance, a suspicious-looking man began to walk behind him. Uday was confirmed that someone, indeed, was tailing him. But he couldn't identify the suspicious man. He guessed that this man could be a Taliban or a possible threat, so, he started to speed his pace in order to escape from his sight. After running for some distance, Uday could no longer spot the man and finally went to his safe house. Uday ran until he reached his house. He quickly opened the door, got in and shut is behind himself. He was panting when his wife, Aishia, looked at him worriedly.

"What happened, Shabaz? Is everything alright?" asked Aishia, is a Syrian local helper for Uday (Shabaz) and he married to Aishia to gain citizenship. Uday has been undercover over 3-4 years and this contractual marriage to a local woman helped him do his work without any problem.

"No, I have been exposed; someone knows my identity," said Shabaz.

"Oh no! What now?" Aishia asked panic-stricken.

"I have to move from here now otherwise you will get into trouble," Shabaz informed.

"No! Wherever you go, I will also come along," Aishia resolved.

"You will not go anywhere!"

"No, whatever happens, we will see."

"No, you have to stay because if anything happens to me or if I die, my country will not accept me and they will delete all my data and presence of mine. So, you have to make promise to me that you have to inform to my family that I am dead. If you love me you have to do please"

"So, what next?" asked Aishia.

"First I need to call my wife."

Then Aishia gave the untraceable cell to Shabaz to call his wife, Pratibha, living back in India with their daughter and son.

"Hello, who am I talking to?" Pratibha answered the call.

"Hello, Pratibha. I am Uday! How are you?"

"Oh my god! After three years we are talking! I am fine. You tell me, how are you?" Pratibha blabbered excitedly.

"Yeah, I called you because I may or may not see you tomorrow. I don't know. If I am not alive tomorrow, you have to call Srivastav and tell him about the *Red alert*"

"What's that? I don't understand—why are you talking like this?" She asked him as worry and anxiety clouded her mind.

"How are Gaurav and Aishi? Are they well? Tell them that I love them a lot and also tell them I am sorry for not being there for them all the time." Uday added after a brief pause, "I will disconnect the call so remember if anything happens to me, call Srivastav and tell him about the RED ALERT!"He disconnected the call and turned to Aishia.

"Thank you for everything and be there for me please. Do me that favour I had asked for."

"Hmm ... It will be my duty and I will do it."

Uday left for his secret hideout without further ado.

Meanwhile, another agent, after several attempts, successfully located Uday. However, by the time he reached, Uday was gone; so was Aishia. So, now once again he was left with no leads.

After looking into the blast, he came to know that the blast was only a test for something big but he didn't know what the big plan was. With the help of his local informer, he learnt that the most wanted terrorist named Abdul Syed was involved in that, functioning right from Syria. He immediately called up the General.

"Rakesh did you find Uday or not?" Srivastav's voice was heard from the other end.

"No, Sir, I got address but there was nobody else by the time I reached. But I got information about the blast, Sir!" Rakesh replied.

"Okay, tell me what is there?"

"The blast was planned and executed by Abdul Syed."

"Ah! The most wanted terrorist—Abdul Syed! If so, then the information is valuable and we will have to take a quick call! "

"It is a reliable source, Sir. I got this information from the local informer. I am ready to take over, sir," Rakesh informed confidently.

"No, wait! If we have to take him down that means we need Air-help perhaps a chopper aircraft because he is brilliant and has got connections. If he at all suspects that we know about him, he can go to any length, so wait. I will call the PM and will ask for the permission for this operation. Wait for my call."

As soon as he disconnected the call, Srivastav got on a call with Tiwari, the PM's PA and requested for an emergency meeting. Tiwari asked him to come immediately as the PM was about to leave soon.

PM Office

"So, General Srivastav, what's the situation now? Is there any progress?" the PM asked.

"We have gathered information from another agent at Syria that—" The PM suddenly interrupted him and said, "you didn't tell me about this other agent."

"No, Sir, such things are extremely sensitive and confidential and we are bound by certain protocols, Sir."

"Right! Tell me, why are you here?"

"This other agent informed us that the blast was done by Abdul Syed."

"You mean the most wanted terrorist?"

"Yes, sir, it is the best chance for us to capture him," said Srivastav.

"How do you wish to do it?" the PM asked.

"We can take the help of local army force, sir. I am confident that they want Abdul Syed just as much as we do! With your permission, we must begin; there is no time, Sir!

"Okay, I trust you with it. All the best, General!"

"Thank you, Sir!"

An hour after the general left the office, the PM called Srivastav "Local army will help us. I have taken the necessary permissions and they have agreed to cooperate with us. So, know that all is in your hand now."

"Great! Thank you, Sir."

Then he called for meeting to discuss the mission, briefing the team about Abdul Syed. Agent Aditi was to lead the team, joined by. Agent Rajesh, who was an Indian Agent who came with Agent Aditi to find Uday. Meanwhile, Aditi contacted Rakesh, the Indian agent from Syria, who was operating under cover for so many years with Uday, and told about the operation so he told Aditi to stay at there at the Indian army base, in India.

15 August 2000,

Aleppo, Syria

As they landed in the Syria, they were picked up by the local army and were taken to thebase. Syrian Army had agreed to provide us with weapons and some of their agents. It is led by agent Amira she is a Syrian Agent who will help the Indian agent to find Uday. And as they got location of the Abdul Syed.

And both the teams of Agent Aditi and Agent Amira were ready to leave for the location. As soon as they reached, they took their positions and carefully approached factory when they heard a voice crying out loud in pain. Agent Amira asked one of her agents to see what it is Through the binoculars, the agent saw someone tied up in a chair, being torturing by some men. When Rakesh heard it from the agent, he suddenly realised that the man is none other than Uday!

"He is one of our agents! So, know that we have two jobs—one is to take down Abdul Syed and the next is to rescue Agent Uday!"

"No! Our deal includes taking down Abdul Syed alone. No more," said Agent Amira sternly.

But he is one of us; we can't leave him here to die! We must improvise our plan and take both of them," Agent Aditi replied.

Agent Amira agreed under the pressure of the situation. The voice that they could hear had stopped. Immediately Amira alerted them as they now could see only the tied person.

"Okay, then Rakesh and I will get Uday. So, Amira and Rajesh will take Abdul Syed," said Agent Aditi.

As soon as they agreed on the next steps, they hurried towards the building. Aditi and Rakesh went for Uday. Before approaching him, they looked around to see if they saw anybody and then quickly they untied him.

Meanwhile, Amira and Rakesh searched room by room but with no result! So, after a while, the entire team returned to the location where Uday was tied.

Seeing them come back, Aditi asked Amira, "Why did you come back? What happened?"

"There is nobody in this building except us," replied Amira.

"But how is that possible? We saw them!" said Rakesh.

A terrifying thought gradually dawned upon Uday. There could be a high chance that an ambush had been set for them. He immediately warned the others—

"Ohio! Guys, we must leave the building ASAP! IT'S A TRAP! RUN!"

Alas! It was too late. Everybody in that building started to have difficulty in breathing, and soon, in a blink of a minute, the entire building exploded into flames before either of the agents could escape their fate.

Delhi, India

RAW Headquarter

General Srivastav got a call from the Syrian local authority, informing that there was a bomb explosion where all his agents got killed. On hearing that, General Srivastav collapsed on the chair in shock. But, as he think about Uday and his friendship with him then he receives the call.

Then he received a call from the Delhi local Hospital, informing him of an explosion in a market somewhere in New Delhi and some lady gave this number to contact him.

"What's her name?" asked Srivastav.

"Her name is Pratibha," replied the doctor.

"I will go and meet her but take care of her and her children," replied the General.

"No, Sir, unfortunately, we could only save the mother; the daughter is dead in the blast. But we didn't tell her about her daughter yet."

Deeply sorry for the agent's family, the General said, "Take care of her; I will be there in 15 minutes." He disconnected the call and was about to leave the RAW building when he got a call from the Syrian branch, informing that one of their teams are dead due to bomb explosion half an hour ago. They expressed their condolences for that and asked the General to collect the bodies General Srivastav was in shock. That's when Tiwari came in and informed that there are apparently two more bombs planted both in Delhi and Syria. General knew that he first had to meet Uday's wife. Without further ado, he went to the hospital and went to see the doctor-in-charge.

"You have to save her, whatever cost it may be—I will bear!" the General declared.

"I'm afraid, we can't do that sir ... she has only a minute. Her breathing condition is very unstabl. She can't hold for that long time. So, whatever is there, this is the best time."

The General entered Pratibha cabin to be shocked to see 90% of her body burnt. Pratibha gestured Srivastav to come closer. When he did, she asked in a quivering, weak voice, "How is Aishi?"

Then Srivastav paused for bit and his eyes were red with tears brimming and then

Pratibha asked, "What has happened to her? Is she alright or not? Tell me, brother!"

"Sorry, Pratibha, they couldn't save her," Srivastav replied.

Then Pratibha started to cry of pain.

Srivastav softly asked, "But, where is Gaurav?"

"I had left him at home with the babysitter; he is fine. Yesterday, Uday had called me and said something about RED alert. Could you help me, brother?"

"Yes, I will. What is it?"

"Take care of my Gaurav…" Those were Pratibha last words before her life gave up. Emotional and grieved by her death, General Srivastav left the hospital and headed towards the Rashtrapati Bhaven.

PM Office

The moment General Srivastav entered his office, the prime minister got up, "What happened? What I heard is true? Has Abdul Syed escaped?"

"Yes, Sir, I am very sorry sir. Now only I know about the RED alert sir."

"What is *RED alert*?" asked the PM.

"It is a code word for betrayal; someone in our agency has leaked confidential information, sir"

"Do you have any idea who it can be?"

"No, sir, we can't find them easily sir. We could have done it but Abdul is now a ghost—we can't find him until he shows himself up," Srivastav sighed.

"Then what can we do?"

"Nothing as of now. Some of our agents are coming from Syria, so, sir, for their family's security we have to do something!"

"Yes! Of course! They do enough for their country and now it's our turn to do something for them"

Then he left the PM office and he finishes all formalities about their agent and about Uday family. After he went to the Uday's house he took the Gaurav in to his house.

As soon as he entered the house, his wife, Anu, asked, "Who is he?"

"He is my friend's son," replied Srivastav.

"And why is he in our house?"

"His family died in a blast that happened at the Mall."

"I still don't understand why he is in our house."

"From now onwards he will live with us as our son, along with our daughter Sakshi," said Srivastav.

Shocked by what she heard, Anu exclaimed, "What! I can't accept him as my son! He is not my son!"

"Anu ... I have to ... because I promised my friend and his wife to look after him!" pleaded Srivastav.

"Fine then! Look after him ... but you can look after him by keeping him in an orphanage too.Wecan meet him once in a while, so, that will good for him as well as for our daughter," reasoned Anu.

"What?! I can't do that! I promised them that I will look after him, so I will keep my promise and I will take care of him right in this house," said Srivastav angrily.

Anu got angry. "If he stays here, I can't live with you!"

"What are you saying? He has no one in his family ... we should try to help him instead!"

"That's what I am saying—we can put him in some orphanage so that we can look after him ... and even visit him once in a while. We can also give him some money to take care of himself."

"No, I can't. He is just a child ... he doesn't know anything about the world and until he grows up, we have to help him by making him live with us."

"So, you will not listen to me?"

After a brief pause, Srivastav replied, "I will look after him as my son in my house and you also accept him as your son, Anu."

"Then you have to choose between your family and that boy."

"What?! What are you saying? I can't..."

"Yes, you have to. If you stay with him then I will leave this house with my daughter right now."

Srivastav was helpless. He definitely couldn't part with his family—his beloved little daughter, Sakshi … He then turned to look at Gaurav, who was standing there in a corner with a small face and eyes glistening in tears. That's it. No, he had made a promise to his friend. He surely couldn't break it now—now when this boy needed him the most. Anu will understand sooner or later … Things will be fine with time. Srivastav made his decision—to keep Gaurav with him.

He said, "No, I can't leave him to any orphanage. I made promised to someone, so, I will raise him as my son."

Anu went to her room and packed her bags, ready to leave with their daughter. Just as she was about to leave, Srivastav blocked her way and tried one last time, "Anu, I love you! Please understand the situation of that boy! I made a promise to my friend!"

"So, you can keep your friends' promise but not me and our daughter," she smirked, "I will come to this house after you leave him at the orphanage," and then she stormed out of the house with the luggage and their daughter before Srivastav could utter a word.

In the meantime, after the blast, that took so many lives in India, all the Law enforcement Officers started to dig the evidences. As they were searching for any evidence in the CCTV footages near the explosion sight, they found that the vehicles belonged to INW Weapon Industry. Those vehicles were parked on the spot a day before explosion, so, the officers began to doubt if the INW Company had any link to this. They soon got the warrant to search their office and all data. After looking at them, they got to know that the CEO of the company had some connection with the terrorist group and other Underworld criminals. Apparently, this CEO was smuggling weapons to the underworld and they also found that the

CEO was the man behind the blast in India. He was also transporting weaponry illegally to the other countries and terrorist groups. After collecting all the documents, the police arrested him and took him to their custody to interrogate him.

On the other hand, somewhere far in the neighbouring country, Abdul Syed forged a fake identity and enter Pakistan where he stayed for a while to buy time. Then he went back to Iran with his family and started planning on his next operation, but this time he was training his sons too.

Chapter 2
GROWN-UP BOYS

2012,

India–Pakistan Border,

Army General RavindSharma got the information from the intelligence bureau that the most wanted terrorist, Abdul Syed, has been hidingsomewherein Iran.

Sharma immediately reported this information to his chief and subordinates and added, "Sir,wehave received a confirmed information, we have to take a call!"

"Okay,then start the mission," ordered the chief.

A proper plan was executed, keeping the PM and the army in the loop. The soldiers were then called to the base. As all of them gathered in the meeting room,thegeneralgreeted them all, "Okay boys, good afternoon to all! Today we are all gathered here because we got the information about the most wanted terrorist—he is back, and according to our sources, he is active now.So we are running short of time and we don't know that he will be their but we have to try,"

General Sharma then started to address and refer to the projector screen to give the information about this Abdul Syed.

"This is the latest photo of Abdul Syed that we could procure. Andit is from back in 2000 when some of our agents had captured that image. Sharma went on to show pictures of his son, Mohammad, whose information were not there in any filessincehe had completely disappeared. He then showed Syed's trusted manHuzaifa Rana's photo if anything Abdul says anything he is the man for that type of job combined these two they totally bombed about 50 and about killed 23000 people are killed and some our brave soldiers and agents"

Having seen the photos and slides, the men said in unison, "Sir,wewilltry our best to take him down!"

"Not try the best—you all *must* bring him down because we have a lot to ask him. Is everybody clear?" General Sharma asked.

The faces of all the soldiers flushed with energy onhearingGeneral Sharma. They grinned and shouted with pumped up adrenaline,"YES SIR! WE WILL BRING HIM DOWN SIR!"

General Sharma replied with satisfaction, "I know boys, you all will make the country proud once again.I trust you, boys!"

After the meeting, the general ordered all the captains to stay back for some further information while the restleft the meeting.

"Okaycaptains, this is in your hands.You have to deal with it!All my superiors have got faith in me and I am relying on you lot—so you all have to have success in the operation!"

Captain Gaurav along withotherssaid, "Sir,yes sir, we will!"

"Right then. We will make threeteams,first team—Team Alpha— will be led by Captain Koushik. They will transport to the location near the camp of Abdul Sayed.The second team—Team Beta—will track Team Alpha's location and it will do ground strike.Beta will be led by our tracking and analysis intelligence officer, Captain Gaurav," he nodded towards Gaurav and continued, "and Captain Sandeep will head the third team—Team Gama—which will be the eyes of the Betateam;and after capturing Abdul Syed, Team Alpha will collect Team Beta from Helicopter and we have to do as per the plan.Nobodycanfail the plan.It is our best chance!We will be monitoring all of your activities, so, if anything bad happens, we will inform you all on the spot,ok captains, all are ready?"

"Sir,yes sir!"

"Okay,you guys make your team ready.You all will leave the base at 0700 hours evening and get ready."

0700 Hours

Pakistan–India border, Katra

According to the plan, team Alpha transported the teams BETA and GAMMA to the location of Abdul Syedcamp,and left the place to the destination point, their safe house near the camp of the Abdul Syed.While Team Gamma led by Captain Sandeep took the roof,Team Beta took the ground led by Captain Gaurav and General Sharma asked Capt. Gaurav to take the lead.

"Okay sir, as I count one—5—4—3—2—1!Move on boys!" ordered Capt. Gaurav.

Each team hadeight members which were divided into two teams of 4 with one of them taking the lead while the other formed the back-up.

"Captain Sandeep,is anything unsuspicious you are seeing?" asked General Sharma.

"Not yet,sir," Sandeep replied as hepeeredthrough the binoculars. Suddenly he noticed something,"Sir,something is wrong … we got movement."

"How many are there?IsAbdul Syed present or not?"

"NoAbdul Syedaround,but about 10 to 20 people are there, sir," Sandeep replied.

"If you sense any threat from them, take a shot," General Sharma said.

"No,sir, it isn't what you think.I will send you live streaming of what I see. You must see it yourself,"and then Sandeep immediately connected to theGeneral. Sharma got surprised by seeing the scene. Then, suddenly, Captain Gaurav contactedhim as well.

"Sir, are you seeing what I am seeing? There is no Abdul or anybody but only hostages, sir! And they have explosions attached to them!"

Frazzled by what he saw, he ordered Capt. Gaurav, "Okay, Captain, quickly free the hostages and see if the explosives can be diffused.I will send ALPHA to pick you viaair;GAMA,cover the BETA until ALPHA comes for you to rescue."ThenGeneral Sharma contacted Captain Kaushik,"Team ALPHA, they need your help,so,leave the destination point immediately and go to the pick-up point.There are about 20 hostages there."

"Sir!" affirmed Capt. Kaushik and immediately left the place with his team on helicopters. Meanwhile, the general contacted both

BETA and GAMMA,

"Okay, teams, ALPHA is on the way to pick you up!"

While Team Beta tried to free the hostages, one of them cried aloud, "In the name of Allah!I will die for my country!" and while saying this, he pressed the button to activate the bomb. The timer showed they had onlyone minute before the explosion.

"Okay, okay, please calm down … there are children and old peoplehere—so please remove the jacket and come with us!"

"They will also sacrifice for their country andALLAH!" said that hostage.

"Don't be foolish!Your god didn't tell you to sacrifice for him; he gave you birth and he only has the right to take that life, not you or that selfish,retard Abdul," spat Gaurav.

Watching this scene unfurl inside, General Sharma quickly contacted Team Alpha. "Team ALPHA, where are you? The situation is getting out of hand—come fast!"

"Within a minute we will be there, sir," said Capt. Kaushik.

"Ohno, there is no time,"then he thought of another plan and contacted Capt. Sandeep.

"Team Gamma, if you have got a clear shot, take the subject down," General Sharma commanded.

"Right, sir, I got a clear shot, sir" Capt. Sandeep replied.

"Okaythen, on my call, take the shot!"

On hearing this exchange of conversation, Captain Gaurav

interrupted them and told to general,"Sir no, it is not a good idea. There are children and old peoplehere and I can't identify the actual bomb sir,they all look different."

"How different? Is it connected to a tube or something liquid captain?"General Sharma enquired.

"It has a tube with green liquid inside, sir," Capt. Gaurav replied.

The General kept raking his brain thinking what this possibly could be when suddenly his operative asked for his permission,"Sir,Gamma is clear to take the shot.What is your call?"

Sharma's mind was still wheeling around the bomb and its nature as he realizedsomething about it whichtook him by complete surprise. He distractedly murmured,"Yaa...yes!"

But unfortunately the operative misunderstood that as an affirmation to hisquestion and gave order to Gamma,"You are clear to take the shot!"

Just then the general heard what the operative toldTeamGamma and he got afraid and saidangrily,"Don't take the shot!"

But it was too late already. TeamGamma had already taken the shot at the terrorist. The general immediately contacted both the teams,"Leave the place immediately!"

Alas! It was too late. One of the bombs exploded.

PRESENT DAY,

Tehran,Iran

In a large area with more people outside the city of Tehran there are groups of people who are giving the training to boys who call themselves ISI agents.

Under the umbrella of theirleader,Abdul Syed, they were all getting trained in various wayswhen suddenly a man came out of a car and asked them to gather for a meeting. They all referred to the man as "Bhai" whose real name was Mohammad Syed, the son of Abdul Syed.After 20 years since that incident in Syria, Abdul had been busy in training his sons to be him.After 2000,Abdul's sonssuccessfully executed several terrorist activitieswithabout a dozen of blastsplanned by the Syed brothers.And now they were planning for something big—nobody could stop them.Theywere training even the children of agetwelve;the locals of that area were afraid of them.

"Whatever you are doing is not good, and God will not forgive any of you!" said Madiha, Mohammad's wife.

"We are doing this for God and in the name of God.You don't tell me about war.Youmust do your job and whatever I tell you to do!Your work is to give birth to children and take care of them and me."

"Don't takeAllah's name and use it for your dirty work!You very well know how many people will suffer from all this," said Madiha.

Mohammad got angry and slappedher.One of their children had seen this and got scared. She immediately took all of her children and went inside,crying.After that, she started to think about what just happened ... then about her children.Shewondered that if she stayed here, it will not be safe forher children or for herself.So, she startedtothink of escaping from that place somehow.

Next morning, a young boy of about 24 years came to meet Mohammad.Thisboy,called Asif, hadascary face with dirt smeared all over.Mohammad took himto the room upstairs to talkinprivate. After a while, the twocame out saying,"Do the work in the name ofAllah and he will do us all good. May He be with you and us!"

After having lunch together,Asif left while Mohammad gathered all his people and addressed them, "Now our enemy will learn about us,that they know that what happens if they declare war against us,"he cried aloud passionately.

Gujarat,India

Present Day,

The man with Mohammad was already in India with the help ofone of their local supporters and he took him to their shelter. In that group, one of the men named Bilal, who worked closely for Mohammad, took him to some other place and there were 4 people like that age and they came from different places they didn't even know each other.

Bilalsaid, "Bhailog, ALLAH will be proud of you and all our Pakistani Bhai Log will be proud of you all you all get 3 days so prepare for yourself,MohammadBhaijaan will make call to move, until you all will stay here,"andBilal left the place and all 5 boys stayed there and started to prepare themselves.

Delhi,India

IATBureau,

After the incident in the year 2000 In Syria,where Uday and other Agents died in that explosion, most of the RAW agents were exposed all over the country and some were killed while some disappeared or were turned over to us and given the information of our agents for the money and some were tortured to give out information.

To control the situation the then PM took a decision to stop most of the intelligence activities and asked them to go underground. After Agent Uday died in the explosion in Syria, the RAW suspected that some insider was leaking the information to the enemy. Immediately, a core team decided to blacklist many agents at that time.

After so many years with our country having gone through innumerable losses, the current PM decided to build a task force which will work under RAW and be an invisible entity, almost non-existent.So, the PM decided to build a secret team and Bureau called IAT—Intelligence Antiterrorist Task and it is an integralpart of the RAW—established in the year 2003andtill date they have succeeded in most of the missions and none of the operations have failed.

Under the leadership of IAT Chief Kulakrni,IAT succeeded inseveralmissionunder him there are 4 agents who will go to any extreme to complete the mission to keep country safe. The chief is successful in all his missions.

Agent Arushi was one of the top agents in weaponry, hand combat and aggression; Agent Varun specialized in hacking like it was a piece of cake;AgentAbhiram specialized in combat and weaponry and extremely sly ininterrogation;Agent Danika specialized in analysing situation,place and person.With these four agents, theChief could do anything,anywhere, at anytime.

Delhi,India

RAW

A meeting was held between all the chiefs of the special units.

"We got information from the Intelligence Bureau that this year there will be attack which we can't even imagine—in fact, there will be bigger attacks so all units should be very alerthenceforth.This message is from the PM so everybody keep an eye; if you see or sense anything suspicious, you have to inform the Bureau ASAP!" said the RAW chief firmly.

"What do you mean by BIGGER ATTACKS?" the IAT chief asked incredulously.

According to IB, there will be more attacks in future. For now we know this much … we don't know what's there planor what's their mission, so, all the best chiefs, be ready for the mission!" the RAW chief completed.

Unknown Area,

NEW DELHI,

IAT,

After the meeting with the RAW, the IAT chief called for an internal meeting with all the agents and analysts are gathered together.

"Guys, RAW called for the meeting about a serious issue," said IAT Chief Umesh Sharma.

"Is there a problem, sir?" asked Agent Arushi.

"Yes, I think it's about our country'ssafety,"Chief replied.

"Is there any attack, sir?" enquired Abhiram.

"Yes, and there will be more attacks, so, be prepared guys.Anytime!" Chief affirmed.

"Yes sir!" the agents cried in unison.

"Danika, you analyse the files of Mohmmad Syed, and Varun track all the calls andkeep an eye.If there's anything you both find suspicious, inform me quickly!"Chief Kulkarni instructed.

Danika and Varun nodded in agreement.

"Where is Gaurav?"asked the Chief.

"Don't know,sir.Since morning Ihave been calling him but he didn't take the calls, sir,"saidAgent Aravind.

Chief thinks for a while and askedAravind, "What's the date today?"

"2nd July, sir," replied Aravind.

"Oh! Right, then he will not come today.Ask him to meet me in my chamber first thing in the morning tomorrow,"the chief said.

"Yes,sir!" said Aravind.

"Sir ... even Danika is there, why him, sir?" asked Arushi.

"Agent Arushi, we are a team that means we are a family, so, please behave yourself," scowled Chief.

After assigning each analyst with their respective responsibilities, the chief called Arushi, Abhiram, Varun and Danika privately in his office for a brief word.

"You four have to keep your eyes open 24/7! I have trust in your team, so, guys keep it in mind—Arushi, you help Varun, and Abhiram, you help Danika!"

The four nodded in acceptance and left for their work.

Next Morning,

IAT,

Since the meeting from the previous day, the entire Bureau was glued to work right from the morning.

"Hey, Aravind! What's happening man? Everybody seems busier than usual, what's wrong?" Analyst Gaurav asked as he entered the office.

"Hey, Gaurav, I had called you so many times yesterday, Where were you? Chief had called for a meeting," said Aravind.

"Why?" asked Gaurav immediately.

"According to RAW and IB, there will be some terrorist attacks. They don't know when or where or even how many attacks, so, Chief has ordered us to work 24/7! Oh! and he also has asked you to meet him at his chamber when you arrive," Aravind briefed Gaurav about the goings-on.

Gaurav immediately headed towards the chief's chamber and as opened the door,a meeting was already going on with Arushi and other teams.He went insideandfound a seat amidst others.After the meeting got over, most of the agents left the chamber, all but Arushi and her team, who stayed back onthe chief's order.

"Alright guys, do you know Gaurav?He works as an Analyst," said Chief Kulkarni.

"Yes,sir, we know him," said Arushi as she exchanged looks with her team and then muttered in a low voice for only her teammates to hear, "and all agents hate him, all except you and his friend Aravind."

"Okay then!He will be your new teammate," informed Chief Kulkarni.

"But sir!We can surely do this by ourselves! We don't want any teammate, especially one who has never been a field agent—"Arushi rebelled.

Taking this personally, Gaurav said, "Right. I think she's correct, Chief. They don't need me clearly. And, to be honest, even I wouldn't want to work with this team."

"Stop it! It is our country that's in danger. We all are teammates and we have to work together to fight against our enemies.So,from now on, Gaurav you have to work with them"

"But sir,if they are not comfortable with me,Icanwork alone as well," replied Gaurav.

"This is my order!Youfive have to work together and that's my final decision. Now go on,continuetokeep atrackon ourcountry.Come on!"

The Chief dismissed all and asked only Gaurav to stay back.

After leaving the chamber,Arushi shrugged and said, "God knows why the chief believes in him so much!"

Abhiram added, "You know, one of our agents got kicked outoff the agency because he provided with the information which we think is false."

"This man is corrupt!Andnow we have to work with him!" cried Varun.

"Oh man!Anyway guys we have work to do,'' said Danika and they soon got involved in their work.

Meanwhile at the chief's chamber, Chief Kulkarni asked Gaurav, "Hmm, so how wasyesterday?"

"I wasn't feeling well, sir ...so,I went to hospital for a check-up," lied Gaurav.

"I know why you didn't come yesterday," said Chief Kulkarni.

"Nothing else sir..."

"Gaurav, you are working with me forsix years—Ihave all information about my agents and I have been watching you since your childhood!So, tell me, how is your mother and your sister Sakshi? Did you speakto them or not?"

"Yesterday was her birthday so I went to see her,butI didn't speak to them."

"Did they know that you were there?"

"I don't think so. I spoke to my father," replied Gaurav.

"Oh! How is Srivastava?Is he well?"

"Yes,he is okay. Because of me they separated … now the family is reuniting after so many years!So,I don't want to ruin their happiness again."

"If you love them, you must go and talk to them about how you feel about them.It is up to you … So, coming back to work, we got business to handle;I need you here," said Chief Kulkarni.

"I will do my best, sir"

"You do realize that your teammates aren't much of your fan, right?So, just be careful."

Gaurav nodded and left the chamber as they got done with their meeting.

Next Day,

Rajasthan,India

Bilal entered the house where all the five boys were staying and said, "*Bhailog*, time has come now show the power of Pakistan to the idiot Indians so much so that it leaves them begging for mercy. MayAllah be with you!"

Transport was arranged as they all packed and set forth towards their destination!

Delhi,

IAT,

While doing normal routine check of all the calls on radio,Gaurav heard something suspicious that got him curious, so, he dug deeper, analysing and tracking the call, **then he gets coded** message from assumedlya terrorist group who were already in India.Shocked by what he heard, he immediately went to meet ChiefKulkarni.

"Chief,you have to see this!" panted Gaurav.

"Is there a problem?"Chief Kulkarni asked, taken aback.

"While doing the routine analysis,Icame across this suspicious message"

"What does it say?"

"Wait, I will show you"then he went to get his laptop and showed it to the chief.

"It was a coded message which I decoded and got surprised," Gaurav began. "In that message, there were two people who were talking with each other—one is named God, the other is Angel," he further explained and turned the screen towards the chief for him to see the exchange of decoded messages:

GOD: Hi ANGEL, how is the work going?

ANGEL: According to the plan.

GOD: It must be going according to the plan.

ANGEL: So what exactly do we have to do, GOD?

GOD: Time is near.

ANGEL: When do we have to land on Earth?

GOD: Enemy is ready or not?

ANGEL: They don't have any idea about this or what is coming.

GOD: OK then, prepare our fighters for the war.

ANGEL: They are all ready,GOD!Youjust give the final call, that's all.

GOD: OK.The festival will be starting on DENSITY so that make sure that plane goes well,"

ANGEL: In the name of Allah!

GOD: MayAllah be with you!

ANGEL:<DENSDWEY129716N775946E C173850N784867ECH 190760N728777EG 287041N771025ERF@4+5>This is the location of your festival.

This was the end of the call. The Chief got surprised as he said,"According to the information, it is very early. This must be informed to theBureau.Okay then, dig deeper to know theirentireplan."

"Sir, first inform the Bureau and call for a meeting, because time is very short," suggested Gaurav.

ChiefKulkarni informed the Bureau,who gave the order to act on it. So, all the units were activated and then Chief called for a meeting in IAT with all the units.

"Guys, according to IB,there is going to be an attack too soon. In fact, we might not have time to take all the desirable measures."

"How can we be sure, Sir?" asked Arushi worriedly.

The chief asked Gaurav to explain all the things to the units.

"Hello everyone! So, as per our investigations, there will be attack an on tomorrow not only in Delhi but also inBangalore,Hyderabad and Mumbai," informed Gaurav.

"How reliable is this information?" asked Arushi.

"While doing the routine analysis I got a suspicious coded message. After I decoded it,I got this—"and he showed the decoded message to them by connecting his laptop to projector.

Arushi along with other agents argued, "There is no suspicious about this message! It's probably some kids' conversation maybe."

"No,it is not.This is a conversation betweenterrorists.See the last line," Gaurav said as he zoomed into the last line.

"What is in it?" asked Arushi.

"They have used word Allah," said Gaurav.

"OKAY. Let's assume this is a conversation between terrorists,but we don't have any evidence of places and where at which time the attack must go on," Arushi went on to reason.

"See clearly—DENSDWEY—after decoding, it showed *WEDNESDAY* and 129716N775946E C173850N784867ECH 190760N728777EG 287041N771025ERF@4+5 means Bangalore: ChinnaswamyStadium;Hyderabad: Charminar;Mumbai:IndiaGate;Delhi: Red Fort; at 4 PM," Gaurav explained.

After hearing everything, Chief Kulkarni said, "then Wednesday is tomorrow, it means at 4 PM tomorrow there will be series ofblasts.

Okay,I will inform the Head of the Department," and then he and the entire team got busy in tracking the location of the call.

Chief calledArushi, Gaurav and the entire team for a meeting.

"Arushi, you and your team have inform the local authority to put check post and check all the vehicles carefully.If this happens, we can't think of the ways in which this will affect our country. Gaurav, go with them and inform about the situation for them," briefed the Chief.

While leaving the office,Gaurav suddenly had a thought which hetoldthe Chief, "Chief, in that message there are some things I didn't understand.Weare missing something, sir!"

"We don't even know whether this information is reliable or not— do we believe in him … is it correct or not,Sir?" said Arushi.

Gaurav shot back, "My information is reliable but I am missing something in this message."

"Okay then, think about it.We have 24 hours' time so think fast. And this information must not get to the media or the public. They will be afraid and get paranoid so keep this asecretanddon't share it with anyone else," The Chief told them strictly.

The rest of the day went by with each of the team members working as per the Chief's orders while Gaurav tried to storm his brain, trying to figure out the missing link to the undeciphered code.Tension creeped in when nothing worked and then he thought of taking help from Srivastava. He made the call quickly.

"What help doyou need? Tell me," asked Srivastava.

"How did you know I called you forhelp?"Gaurav asked, taken

aback.

"Ihave brought you up," Srivastava reminded.

"Hmm … I can't come to your place and my place isn't safe, so, meet me at our hideout within 30 minutesplease.It is urgent!" said Gaurav.

Srivastavamade up an excuse to have some work at the bakery(which he ran after retirement) in front of his wife and left immediately.

Outskirts of Delhi

Hideout,

Night 9:00

As it was late night Srivastavareachedthe hideout exactly in 30 minutes but Gaurav wasn't there yet. As he went inside, he heard a car stopand through the window he saw Gaurav get out of the car. Hequickly went to open the door.

"What is so urgent?Why did you call me at this time?"asked Srivastava.

"Firstlet'sgoinside,I will explain," Gaurav said as he looked around to check if someone is watching them or if someone followed them. After he was sure that nobody was there, he went inside and closed the door.

"Okay, go on … tell me what's happening," enquired Srivastava.

Gaurav began to explain, "A week before, IB clarified that this year there will be more attacks, and after a week, while doing daily routine analysis,Icame across a suspicious coded message.So,I decoded it and found out that it was about some terror attacks and its time and place.I immediately informed this to the chief that the attack will be on Wednesday,which is tomorrow.He has alerted all the units and has informed the Department as well."

"What?!There will be attacks tomorrow??" asked Srivastava, completely shocked.

"Yes, I figured it out and told them."

"So, what are we doing here? What's the plan?" asked Srivastava.

"I think I am missing something but don't know what it is.There is no time,so,Ineed your help to crack it,"Gaurav finished.

"Okay, show me the code,I will see if I can crack it or not," said Srivastava.

The two got engrossed in cracking the code so much so that they lost the track of time.

The next morning he got a call from the chief informing thathe has to meet him, in 15 minutes.

Gaurav disconnected the call and said, "Alright then, I got to go now.You try to figure it out and call me."

"Right, I will call if I find something."

Gaurav left for the IAT headquarter while Srivastava went to his bakery.

IAT Headquarter

Gaurav entered the Chief's chamber to find Arushi and the rest already settled in there.

"Did you figure out the missing code?You see, time is short and according to your information all fivecitieshave been given tight security.I really believe in you!" said Chief Kulkarni.

"Umm … no, I will find it shortly. Please give me some more time," Gaurav requested.

"Okay guys, all you have to go to RedFortand seal it,so, be careful and be attentive!They might already be there so check all the vehicles,persons and placessurroundingit.Okay?Go on!" the Chief ordered and they all headed forRedFortin search for the explosives.

RedFort,

Old Delhi,

"Are you sure we are not wasting time?Wehave searched for it one whole day but gotnothing!Is your information even reliable or not?" asked the local police inspector to Agent Arushi.

"Please do your work as you're told and cooperate with us" snapped Arushiangrily.

Time: 3:55PM,

RedFort,

The day of the attack arrived. RAW took all the precautions to save the country from the attack but they still didn't know much about the exact location of the bomb.

RAW already sent out directives to all the major cities to be under high alert.

All the RAW agents and local law enforcement team were already at the main area of the city, including Red Fort, other tourist spots, airport and railway stations.The IAT agents and few other local police gathered at the Red Fort as the place attracted too many tourists from across the country and the world.Each of the agents were on a lookout for any suspicious people or thing. Some manned the exit and entrance while the others covered from inside. As the time passed, the agents began to getconfused.After quite some time, Gaurav came outside and his eyesfixed on a man who looked suspicious to him. He immediately informed to the local police to watch him and eventually try to stop him from entering the Red Fort. Following orders, the local police shouted at him but the suspicious man kept walking, like he didn't hear them. Unable to control, Gaurav himself began running behind him, to stop him. That's when he receiveda call from Chief Kulkarni.

"Yes, sir?" panted Gaurav.

"Explosions have already occurred in the other major cities, so, be prepared for it,Gaurav.The attack can be any minute now."

"Okay, sir, we will be."

"Sir,wehave got hold of the bomber but we didn't get the bomb sir.He was not carrying a bomb,sir.He only said that he has a bomb,"Arushi told Chief Kulkarni.

 "how can you believe that he is the terrorist may be it coincidence", Chief replied

"yes, thats also possible sir but after seeing the CCTV when he came he has a bag in his hand and after few minutes later when comes out he doesn't has any bag with him", Arushi replied

"ok, then Bring him to our custody.We will interrogate him," Chief replied.

"Okay sir, we will," said Arushi, but Gaurav was thinking something else—there was something wrong.

4:24PM,

RedFort,

Delhi,

Gaurav got a call from the Srivastava, who said, "I have figured out the missing code!"

"That will be not required, they have got the bomber," Gaurav replied.

"That is suspicious…" murmured Srivastava.

"Tell me, whatdidI miss?" asked Gaurav.

"Listen, each city will explode 5 minutes each explosion",

As soon as he heard that, Gaurav started to run inside the Red

Fort. But it was too late. Right at 4:25 PM, there was an explosion. The whole place blew up. Such was the force that the phone fell off his hands.Srivastava turned cold as he knew it had happened. However, a few minutes after, everything gathered themselves and got up. All around they could only see bloodied bodies lying strewn. There was no trace of the bomber. The agents looked at each other helplessly as they saw the dead eyes looking up at them from the ground. They had failed; miserably.

Chapter 3
FROM FOREIGN LAND

Ten Days Before the Explosion in India,

Aleppo,Syria

A mysterious landed in Syria just 10 days before the explosion that had happened in India.He met some people who were part of a terrorist group and they all wentto**Aleppo** city in a car.

As they entered Aleppo is a city in an Syria, there was a routine security check.Their guns and weapons were hidden in the trunk ofthe car so the police couldn't find them.When the police officer came to their car to check the trunk, one of the men in the car showed the copa card with a dollar symbol and handed it over to him. He asked the cop to show it to his superior. As soon as the senior officer saw the card, his face drained off all colour and beads of sweat started to appear on his forehead. In a broken, quavering voice he said, "As-salamualaykum,bhaijaan."

The man replied with a smile,"alaikumsalam."

Thesenior officer ordered the cop,"Leave that car."

"Okay,sir."

While leaving, the man called the police officer and gave him some cash and said,"MayAllah bless you. Take the money and enjoy!"

They entered a small village and went to their leader's superior house. As the man entered the house, a dozen of armed men greeted him.

The man came to Syria to attend a function in this village. He had a nice chat with all the other men and they had dinner together. Later at night, a man named Zorawar knocked at the door of the man's room.

"What I had told you about, is that ready or not?" the man asked on seeing Zorawar.

"Yes, bhaijaan. It was ready as soon as you gave us the green signal," Zorawar replied.

"Okay, I want to see them," the man demanded.

"Okay, bhaijaan. In the morning I will make you meet them. You must now take rest, bhaijaan."

Next Morning,

Zorawar came to the village with a van inside which were a dozen of boys about the same age around 20–25 and all were taken to the some secret place blindfolded. After an hours' journey, they reached the terrorist camp with a 100 terrorists practising their skills. Some of them took the boys to a room and opened their eyes. As soon as they opened their eyes they took in their surrounding and a bad smell hit their nose. The boys got afraid and scared.

Zoravar and the mysterious man entered the room greeted them, "As-salam alaykum, bhailog!"

In scared, quivering voices they all greeted them back, "alaykum salam."

By the look on the boys' faces, the man realized how scared they were and so he started to speak, "Bhailog,you all know why you are here and why I am here.What you're going to do in future is not an ugly work. In fact, even the army and all soldiers do the same but the only difference is that they work under set rules and protocols but we don't have any rules and protocols.It is like you all are doing a great favourto the country.Now time has come for our enemy India to show what we are and who we are, so, guys—don't get afraid and Allah will protect you."

This group also had the five boys who were behind the blast that killed innocent Indian lives. After all the information was briefed, they assigned a job for all the boys.After that, the man finally greeted those five boys.

"In the name of Allah,you all will win and sacrifice for your country. May Allah appreciate you all ... Inshallah!"

The man left the room while Zorawar stayed with the boys.

Delhi,India

NextDay After the Explosion,

RAW,

The RAW called for a meeting to discuss the explosion that took place.

"What went wrong?We were very careful!What happened there?" asked the RAW chief.

"Sir,   we   missed   something   ...   but   we   managed tostopfourexplosionsacross the country, sir," said IAT Chief Kulkarni.

"Yes I know, but after this blast the public are outraged and the media is firing at us and PM is not satisfied with this either; he is blaming me!" the RAW Chief said indignantly.

SFU, another unit under RAW, was also present at the meeting. Their chief added, "Because of their negligence this hashappened,sir. They didn't got reliable source they only predicated it sir,because of this today this happened",

Okay, I will take the responsibility for this, sir, but our prediction was right. It was because of a small mistake that this happened,"Chief Kulkarni reasoned.

"Sir, I think our agents will take this very seriously.So,I want you to transfer this mission to SFU.We would be glad to take thisuphereon, sir," the SFU Chief said confidently.

"Sir, I know we made a mistake, but our resources are reliable.I will not disappoint you next time,"Chief Kulkarni negotiated.

"Sir, sorry to interrupt, but I think it would be only fair to give our unit one chance too. Our team, I'm sure will not disappoint you," said the SFU Chief.

"This is not some competition, it is about our country,so,all the units must work together and share their resources with one another.I think IAT has got good resources,so,let the mission be handled by IAT while other units will cooperate with them,"the RAW Chief affirmed.

SFU, however, wasn't much satisfied with RAW's decision but anyway agreed and then left for their respective offices.

IAT Headquarter,

Soon after the meeting was over,ChiefKulkarni called for an urgent meeting in his office with his team.

"Alright guys, the RAW and our prime minister is very disappointed with the bomb explosion. Because of a small mistake, so many lives were killed ... this can't happen next time," he then looked at Gaurav and called him out, "hey Gaurav!" but he didn't respondfor quite some timeas he looked lost. It was onlyafter several more calls and a few nudges from his teammates that Gaurav returned to his surrounding and quickly replied,"Yes, sir?"

"Are you alright? Is something wrong or what?" the Chief asked worriedly.

"No,sir, everything is alright," Gaurav replied nonchalantly.

"Okay then, we have got bigger attacksinfuture and I think this was some sort of awarning.So, we have to be ready for further attacksand have to stop them. Tell me, guys,anyinformationabout our five dead terrorists?"Chief Kulkarni enquired.

"According to the forensic test results, the five terrorists took their ownlives.Seems like they were quite prepared to get caught and had everything planned out," said Arushi.

"Sir,in all probability, they all are from Syria because the security camera at theAleppoInterntionalairport has captured them entering the airport. Further probing into those profiles, we got their travel details. They all hold Pakistani passports," informed Varun.

"Danika, did you find anything suspicious about them or their family and their background?" asked the chief.

"They all completed electrical engineering in some local institute, sir. Nothing about their family—I will still try to figure it out," Danika replied. The chief then asked them to leave the chamber and continue with their work. He requestedGaurav to stay back for a word.

"I know what you have beenthinking.It is really not your fault," the Chief said.

"It is my fault!Ishouldhave known the message, chief. Because of me, there were so many people who got killed in that bomb blast!" Gaurav said, looking pained.

"This isn't the time for being sorry.This is the time **to rise and work harder.**We can't afford any more mistakes.Go now and get to work by morning.I want all the information about those five terrorists as well as any information about further attacks."

Tehran,Iran

A man came runningtoMohammad's house in a state ofurgency.His face had shock and fear written over it as he said,"Bhaijaan,mission wasn't successful…"

"Hmm … then contact Bilal and Zorawar and tell them about the Diwali gift to our enemy,"Mohammad replied.

"Okay,bhaijaan,"the man said and then then he left the place.

Mohammad then began to call the man who had recruited the boys from Syria, "Bhaijaan,did you know that the mission wasn't successful?"

"Don't you worry, go on with the next gift to our enemy.I will see," the man on the other end of the call replied calmly.

"Okay,bhaijaan,as-salamalaykum."

"Alaykumsalam."

The call was disconnected.

H"N"O"N"I"Fine!" Gaurav finally gave in andThe two began to talk and have dinner together when Srivastava carefully put it before Gaurav, "Come now, , tell me"ISee Gaurav, in a war, sometimes we win and sometimes we lose. And in case we lose, we must not let that pull us down but instead try to prepare ourselves to be even better and work on our mistakes that made us lose! And if we win,;

"HDelhi,India

IAT,

After hours of digging into all the files on those boys,Gaurav had no luck infindinganything.He got frustrated and started to think about the blast and felt sorry for the lives which were taken mercilessly. Just then Srivastava called.

"

ey, what's up?Did anything come up or not?"Srivastava asked.

o, I can't think ... because of me, those people were killed in that blast…" Gaurav trailed off.

kay,meet me in the bakery now.I am waiting for you," Srivastava replied.

know you've got a lot of …lot of work… just come and meet me," Srivastava insisted.

oway!Ican't,I've got lots of work!" Gaurav replied.

went to the bakery to meet Srivastava.

go on

what is your problem?"

ow are they—mother and sister?" Gaurav asked.

 could have found that message earlier … had I done so,there might not have beenany attack or dead bodies,' Gaurav said in agony.

"remember that war is not over

be ready for the next one.Now stop think about losing and think about how to win. Come on, finishyourdinner.I have to go home early today otherwise you know that they will get paranoid," Srivastava winked.

"They are alright."

"You know, after all that I havelost,I am left with only the three of you …what can I do to make things better?" Gaurav asked in plea.

"Umm … for once, talk to them and see how they feel about you,"

"Some other time maybe."

"Knowing you, you will never talk. They will never know about how you feel. You have to take a decision very quickly," Srivastava said.

While talking, they finished their dinner and Srivastavashut his bakery and both went to their respective houses.

After entering home,Gauravstraightaway went for the bed but when he closed his eyes he only saw dead bodies from that explosion.He tried to sleep but he couldn't.His thoughts then wandered to his real mother and sister. Sleep seemed to be a distant reality. After a while, he gave up and then started to work.Hewent through all the files that were associated to the bombing for sometime.Hehad only one lead—Syria—all five of them were from the same place, that is,Syria.He wanted to comb through all the files in details but that wasn't possible for him to do alone, so, he calledArushi and her team at midnight.

"Hello? Who is this?"Arushimumbled sleepily.

"Ineed you and your team now," Gaurav said.

"Do you even know the time? Please don't waste time and go to sleep," said Arushi,irritated.

"I am serious. I want you and your team—especially Varun and Danika—it is urgent!" Gaurav insisted.

"Okay fine!We will be at office in half an hour.Be there."

"Right!I will inform chief about this.You people come," he hung up and contacted the chief and got the permission to work the night with the team.

After half an hour, they all had assembled at the office and found thatGaurav was already there engrossed in work.

"So, tell me what is it? It better be important!" snapped Arushi.

"Well, we have got only one link about this group—that is Syria," Gaurav pointed out.

"What's new inthat?We also know! Is that why you have called us at midnight?!" glared Abhiram.

"Guys, after going through theirfilesI came across something that's common among them, that is, they all have studied in the same college, and have also been recruited to the same software company during campus recruitment."

"What?B-butthat's not therein our file," said Varun.

"I have friends and contacts in Syria who gave me this information," said Gaurav.

"Did you informthisto sir or not?" asked Arushi.

"But it is about the country!There is no time for protocol, please keep this aside.We want evidence.Just while going through this, I saw the name of the samesoftware company!" said Gaurav.

"So,what's in it?Maybe they were just selected in the company," suggested Danika.

"Okay, if they selected for the company, why would they be involved in such terrorism?" asked Gaurav.

"You know, all these terrorists ... they do work not for money but for their jihad!" Arushi said and rolled her eyes.

"Well, what you think is correct … but there is a surprise for you all," said Gaurav.

"What's that?" asked Danika.

"There is nocompany called Intelligence," informed Gaurav.

Arushi and Abhiram together cried at the same time, "What!"

"Wait …I will check it out," he logged into his account and did a bit of research through restricted websites and finally confirmed, "Oh yeah!There is no such company at all."

"Yup. I have already checked; there is no company," said Gaurav.

"That means they were recruiting from a fake company," said Arushi.

"Yes," Gaurav replied,and then their chief suddenly interrupted them as he entered the chamber.

"Did you get anything, guys?" asked Chief Kulkarni.

Arushi told him about how they recruit people to a fake company. On hearing this, Chiefsaid, surprised,"How did you find this? It was never in our file!"

"Ask Gaurav," said Varun.

"It's him?Okay then, what did you find?" the Chief asked.

"Give me time until morning,chief,I will definitely get something," Gaurav replied.

"Okay, if you get anything, call me. I will give you alltimetill morning," said the chief as he left the office to him and went back to his house.

Next Morning,

Tehran,Iran

Mohammad was busy with his terrorist group. They were planning for the next attack while the house and its perimeters were constantly being guarded by armed men.

Ali and Zoya, children of Mohammad and Madiha, got afraid by lookingatthem—headswrappedwithturban,facesfull of bruises and long,unkemptbeard.The man walked to the boy that the others were sitting around, and then, all of a sudden, this turbaned man started to beat up the boy ruthlessly. Seeing the boy's blood spill around, the children got terrified and began to shiver.

But this was something they had seen before. After watching them for some time, they got used to their presence and soon the fear turned into boredom.So,Ali and Zoya thought of playing football because Ali liked the game andZoyacouldn't deny her brother. As they started playing on the terrace, Ali used all his might in kicking the ball and,as a result, the ball fell down.Zoya scolded her brother for hitting the ball so forcefully, "Ali,can't you play nicely and gently?You wait here,I will bring the ball."

Zoya went to fetch the ball but as she reached the ground, the ball was nowhere to be seen.She kept searching for iteverywhere.Then, suddenly, a man appeared, holding their ball in his hand.By seeing his pockmarked and bruised face,Zoya got scared.Hewent near her and started assaulting Zoya.Zoya was trembling with fear when she heard Ali's voice from behind,

"Sister, where are you? Did you found the ball or not," Ali asked.

As soon as the man heard Ali's voice, he turned to have a look at him. He then handed the ball to Ali with a smile that was sly.They got the ball and Zoya ran inside the room, calling for her mother, "Ammi, where are you?"

The tone of Zoya's voice scaredMadihaas she wondered if something had happened to her daughter.She saw Zoya running towards her.

"Why are you crying,Zoya?What has happened?"

"Ammi, I am afraid of these people out there ... who are they?What are they doing in our house?Whyisn'tAbbu telling them anything?" Zoya asked while sobbing.

Madiha hugged her children and cried silently, careful enough for children not to notice her crying. She said,"they all are your Abbu's friends."

"What type of friends,Ammi?I don't want stay here ... please take us away from here,Ammi," Zoya cried.

Mohammad suddenly entered the room. Aisha looked atthe children and said, "Go to your room and stop crying."

"What is withthechildren?Are they fine?" Mohammad asked.

"They got scared of all that has been happening outside,please leave this work,"Madiha pleaded.

"What we are doing is for our people and we have to teach them a lesson so that in future they don't bother us," said Mohammad.

Oy hearing this, she got scared and turned around and saw her children and saw them, their eyes full with fear, and finally decided to escape from that place.

Delhi,India

IAT,

After the blast the bodies were taken to the unit as the forensic were search for the belongingsof the bodies they found Mobile phones form there bags, and as they checked the mobile they comes to know that they used an anonymousprivte messaging website to conversation with an Unknown ID, and as they looked into the chat they start to doubt that these are sucide bomber.

And as they look into the unknown ID they tracked that unknown ID and that ID belongsto the name Billal who is the man of Mohammadd.

While checking information about the man named called Bilal and he the middle man to Mohmmad who will take the order from Mohmmmad when they searching for the boys they come across Bilal who will take care of the money of those boys who were suicide bomber and any local files that were linked with syria he got an suspicious information about the terrorist group so he told the information to chief,

"Chief, we have to call for a meeting and inform this to RAW," said Gaurav.

"Did you find anything?" asked Chief Kulkarni.

"Yes, I've got something toinformtheRAW chief; there is no time!"

The chief agreed and immediately contacted RAW and a meeting was fixed.ChiefKulkarnialso called Arushi and her team along with Gaurav to the RAW Headquarter.

RAW Headquarter,

"Kulkarni, is there anything that you and your boys found out?" asked the RAW Chief.

"Yes,sir,we have got one solid evidence, sir," replied the IAT Chief.

"What's that?" asked the RAW Chief.

The IAT chief went on to show the information to all in the projector,

"What is this? Is this the statement of the local bank of Syria? What's in there?"asked the RAW Chief.

Gaurav began to say something but Arushi stopped him, "Gaurav, sir is talking now, you keep quiet," she said through gritted teeth.

Without paying any heed, Gaurav interrupted them, "They are not just bank statements, sir."

"Who is this,Kulkarni?" asked the RAW Chief.

"Sir, he is the one who got the lead about this and he is our analyst— Gaurav."

"Okay Gaurav,go on … what's this about?" the RAW Chief said.

"Sir,afterarresting those five boys,Istartedresearchingon their history.That's when I found a common link between each of them," Gaurav explained.

"What's that?"

"Sir, all these five boys are from same country, Syria."

"Anything else in common?"

"There is lot in common among them, sir."

"Go on."

"Sir,they studied from the same local college and were recruitedby the same company.All those boys are electrical engineers,"Gaurav said as hepresented all the documents to the people atthemeeting.

"What's in that?Could be a coincidence," said the SFU Chief.

"Sir,in this line of our work we don't believe in coincidence. Wejusthave to believe and think," replied Gaurav.

Everybody started smiling as the SFU Chief got embarrassed.

"Right,go on Gaurav," said the RAW Chief.

"So, they are linked with one person,a man namedBilal, whomthey contacted before entering India.While they had checked into Syria airport, that clip was captured in CCTV," said Gaurav, as he played a video, and then continued,"but the interesting point is that,sir,theydon't even know each other.After they all left Syria, they were found inthedifferent cities of India."

"But this is not too strongalead,Gaurav," said the RAW Chief.

"Wait sir,here is the most interesting point—after all this information,IrealizedthatSyria has been the common factor in all this,so,I put a surveillance on Syria.Ourteamthenstarteddigging deeper and then we came to know thatsome kind of bank transactionshave been going on for a long time, sir."

"How can you say that thesetransactionshave been done by the terrorists?"

"The amounthas been transmitted to the account holder by the name Saifaz."

"You mean the account and all resources holder,Saifaz, is the resourceful person and he is the investorfor terrorists?"

"Not that, also, sir, he is the budget manager of the most important group called Taliban."

On hearing this, everybody at the meeting stiffened and gasped, whispering among themselves.

"So,you mean, behind the last bomb attack, theTalibanwere involved," the PM spoke up for the first time.

"No,sir,Idon'tthinkit's them this time," said Gaurav.

"Why? You just mentioned that the man connectedtoTaliban is linked to the bomb blast. Then what is it?" asked the PM curiously.

"I don't think so, sir," said Gaurav.

"Please be more precise and clearer—who is actually behind these?" asked the SFU chief impatiently.

"Yes, I think we have to make a move," replied the PM.

"Sir,if we make a move and then learn that the attack wasn't planned bythe Taliban, then what sir?" Gaurav pointed out.

"Yes, sir,Gaurav has a point.What do you think then Gaurav?" said the RAW Chief.

"For now, we must work ontracking and keeping a close eye on this link, sir," opined Gaurav.

"Which means Syria," added the RAW Chief.

"That's correct.According to the data of all the transactions, we see that onthe 2nd week of every month, on the same date—13th— there is a transaction.So, we've got about 24 hours until the next transaction," Gaurav calculated.

"Are you suggesting we have to go to Syria?" asked the RAW Chief.

"Yes,sir, we have to!If we miss this then we won't have time left because the amount transferred is thrice the budget that were used in the 26/11 attack,sir.With this amount, they can do bigger and far worse attacks like 26/11 and what not!Sir, please, this is our last chance.Ifwe capture him,atleast we will come know about the upcoming attacks sir."

"PM sir,this is the chance.Please give us the order, sir," requested the RAW Chief.

The PM thought for a second and then gave hisorder, "Alright then, but which team will take it up?"

then SFU unit chief gets up says,"our team will go sir we are best chance sir",

The RAW Chief speaks up, "I think PM sir, the IAT will have to handle it under Chiefl Kulkarni."

"Okay then, IAT will handle this case. And all the units will work under IAT. That's sorted then!All the best for the mission! I will contact the Syrian administrator and inform about the mission," said PM and left the headquarter.

"Kulkarni,I got a feeling that your teamisreliable.I think you will do well," said the RAW Chief.

"Yes,sir!We will!" said Chief Kulkarni enthusiastically.

"Okay guys, good luck,andGaurav—congrats for the work!" said the RAW Chief smiling at Gaurav.

"It is not just me,sir;our team made this possible," Gaurav replied, gesturing towards his entire team.Arushi and her team were quite taken abackwith surprise and thanked him for mentioning them.

"Guy,all the best!TheRAWChief believes in us, so, be careful about this mission. Now go andget some rest. Be prepared to have your busiest days from tomorrow onwards," Chief Kulkarni said.

They all left and walked towards the parking lot. Arushi suddenly stopped and told Gaurav, "Hey thanks for acknowledgingus as a team."

"It's our duty.We all are a team and if any one of the team members does the work, it is considered that the work is done by the team. You seem team is not made up of one person, it is a group of friends. So ... can we have dinner asagreatteam?" asked Gaurav. He further added, "I have a special restaurant perfect for tonight!Let'sall go there."

As they all agreed, Varun asked, "Is their food good there?"

"They have a good chef," Gaurav replied.

Gaurav took them to the place owned by Srivastava and before reaching, he dialled him up, "Hey father, there will be guestsat our cafetonight.Prepare for the chef's specials!" Gaurav said happily.

"Oh great! Bring them soon, we all will have a good time.By the way, Sakshi is also here with her friends, come fast!" Srivastava said.

Gaurav got very excited on hearing that Sakshi was also there at the bakery. He replied, "Okay! Coming as fast I can."

Arushi, who was listening to Gaurav speak on the phone, said, "Ah! Your father runsabakery here?"

"Yes!" Gaurav replied.

As soon as they reached the bakery, Srivastava greeted them with a broad smile, "Hello guys!Pleasefeel comfortable and I will be back in a minute."Heserved them some drinks and left.

"Guys, wait here.I will be back," Gaurav excused himself as they settled down. He then walked tothe table whereSakshi and her friends were seated.

"Hi Sakshi, how are you?" Gaurav asked softly.

On hearing her name, she turned around to see who it was. The moment she saw his face, shegotfurious and said, "Why are youhere?You know that I hate to see your face!Because of you, my mother and father got separated.Now, after so many years, they arefinallyhappy.Don't you darecome back in our life!"

She went on insultinghiminfront of everyone and then called her father, "It's you who has called him,na?" she snapped.

"No … no … it is not father's fault.I only came here … please don't blame him!" Gaurav said.

"Sakshi!He is your brother!What are you saying?" said Srivastava angrily.

"He is not a brother to me! Because of him you and mother got separated!I hate him for that!" she said and snapped at Gaurav and said,"Onceagain,I am warning you—don't ever come near my family.We are not your family!" and then she stormed out of the bakery with her friends following her.

Feeling devastated, Gaurav went over to his team and sat for a while. But almost immediately excused himselfandwent to the balcony.Arushi, who had heard and seenthe whole scene,followed him to the balcony and asked softly,"Is he not your father?"

This pissed Gaurav off as he replied, "Who said?He is my father and she is my sister and they are my family!"

Srivastava then entered the balcony, came closer to him andsaid,"You know how is she—let it go..."

"You also very well know thatbecauseof me you all got separated, so she blames me forthat.She hatesme.Now I have you, only you!" said Gaurav.

"What about us,man?We are not only a team, we are also likeafamily.Don't you ever think you're alone!" said Varun with a smile on his face.

"Okay, thank you, guys!" replied Gaurav.

"Come on! I am starving now!Can we start eating?Because tomorrow ... you know right?"

They all started dining together whenSrivastavaaskedGaurav, "What's tomorrow,eh?Isitanything from work?"

Everybody stopped eating and exchanged glances. One of them said, "No sir, tomorrow we have to go to London toattendsomeseminar. That'sall."

"Guys, he knows about me and what I do," said Gaurav and then they all looked at him in surprise. He went on to add, "moreover, he himself was in army, served the nation as the General!"

"Ooh! We didn't know that, sir,"Arushi said, impressed.

"Come on now, what's going on tomorrow?" Srivastava asked impatiently.

"Is this place safe enough to discuss such matters?" asked Arushi, interrupting them.

"Good point," said Gaurav.

"Okay, wait. We have billed for the last table. Let them leave, then we can resume," said Srivastava and then he got up, walked towards the table with the only guests remaining at the café. He wished them night and collected the bill. The moment they left, he pulled the shutter down and hurriedly got back to their table.

Without wasting another minute, Gaurav began, "From the attack that happened a few days ago, we have traced a link to Syria.So, after an extensivemeeting with the PM and RAW, they haveacceptedthe link. Hence,we are all going to Syria tomorrow."

"What?!Syria?" asked Srivastava, completely shocked.

"Why?What happened?" Gaurav asked confusedly.

"You know that I don't like that country.Your da——"

Gaurav cut him short and said,"YesI know my father got killed in that country, but now I can take care of myself."

"But youhave a desk job!Then why are you involving yourself in a field job?" asked Srivastava angrily.

Gaurav"Youknow me ... I will take care of myself," Gaurav assured.

"Hmm, I know you," said Srivastava hesitantly.

They all finished their dinner and badeSrivastavagoodbye. Srivastava suddenly stopped Arushi.

"Arushi, wait—I have to talk to you!"

"What, sir?" asked Arushi.

"Please look after him for me please, will you?"Srivastava requested.

"Of course,sir!We area team,"Arushi replied.

"Best of luck for your mission!"

"Thank you, sir! We'll see you soon."

After they all left the cafe,Srivastava and Gaurav cleaned the place and locked the gates. On their way back home,Srivastava told Gaurav, "Gaurav, take care of yourself."

"Don't worry about me. You keep sister and mother safe,okay?"

Once home, Gaurav started to think about what happened at the cafe.Sakshi's words were echoing in his ears as sadness engulfed him and he started thinking about her real sister and mother.

Next Morning,

IAT Headquarter,

Arushi, Gaurav and the entire team had reported at the IAT Headquarter just on time. The RAW and IAT chiefs were also present.

"Alright guys, theSyrian authorities have agreed to help us and they have also agreed to arrange vehicles and support to you. we already contacted them.Theconveyancewill be in 12 hours so you have leave know once again best of luck", said the RAW Chief.

"Okay,thank you sir," said Arushi.

The team was about to board the plane whenKulkarniwent to them and said, "Guys, we all are expecting the best from you,especially from youGaurav.Okay?"

The team shouted in unison, "YES SIR!We will!"

The plane took off from the Indian soil.

After a while,Arushi told Gaurav, "Your father is worried about you very much.You know that, right?"

"Yeah, he worries too much," replied Gaurav with smile.

Varun and Danikalooked at Gaurav and said, "Yesterday's dinner was absolutely delicious!Thanks for that!"

"Well, if we accomplish this mission, there will be another dinner!Okay guys?" Gaurav winked and everybody laughed in joy.

Chapter 4
ACTION ON FOREIGN LAND

Syrian Army Private Airport

1700 hours

After hours of flight they finally reached the Syrian Army private airport whereSyrianlocal police were already waiting for them.As they landed in the Syria,the SIU agents were already waiting for them under the guidance of Agent Derifa and Agent Abbas hey both greeted Arushi, Gaurav and their team,

SIU Syrian Intelligent Unit is an sub unit of MID which will work under MID.

"Welcome to Syria guys, I am agent Derifa and he is agent Abbas from SIU.We will be your help as long as you all are here."

"Thankyou very much," said Arushi and went on to introduce all her teammates—Varun, Danika, Abhiram and Gaurav, as well as herself from IAT India.

"We have arranged your stay at a private hotel.Youall must go and freshen up.Then at dinner we can discuss the mission," said Derifa.

They IAT squad left for the hotel in the car arranged by the SIU Agents.

Sheraton Hotel,

Aleppo,Syria

As they walked towards the elevator, Varun said cheekily, "You noticed the agent or not,Abhiram?"

"What?" asked Abhiram.

"Hey didn't you notice Agent Diana?Sheis very beautiful,eh?" winked Varun.

"Don't you have any manners at all, Varun?" snapped Danika.

"Why?" asked Varun innocently.

"Why? You have a girlfriend!And you're talking about thisDerifa" said Danika.

"I only expressed how she looks. You also know how much I love my girlfriend,"Varun defended.

"You have a girlfriend!" exclaimed Gaurav.

"Why?You don't have any?" teased Varun.

"Forget about me—what about Arushi and Abhiram?" asked Gaurav.

Before Arushi could reply, Varun said, "Arushiis married and has two children, and Abhiram just got married!"

"Ohreally?Arushi, you are married!My bad luck!" he joked and continued,"and what about youDerifa?"

"No, I don't have anyone," Danika replied.

"Don't you feel bad …we are on the same boat!" consoled Gaurav.

As they reached their rooms,Arushireminded them, "Guys, tomorrow sharp at 6:00 PMwe will meet at the lobby,okay?"

Sheraton Hotel,

Aleppo,

0600 Hours

Derifa and Abbas were already waiting at the lobby and after a few minutesArushi and her team joined them.But Gaurav was nowhere to be seen.

DerifaaskedArushi, "Where is your other agent?"

"Let's wait, he will be here any moment," replied Arushi.

Gaurav came in after five more minutes.AgentDerifa got angry because he was late, "Do youknowwhat the time is? You're late!"

"I'm sorry guys, but I am late by onlyfiveminutes.What's the harm?"

"Oh, so you are five minutes latef!" scowled Agent Arushi.

"Okay madam, this will not happen again. I am sorry," said Gaurav.

A few minutes later, Gaurav entered the lobby and joined the team. Derifaalong with the team then left for the SFU bureau headquarter.

While in the car, Varun and Gaurav started whispering between themselves in hushed tones, "Ooh, man, she is not only gorgeous, but she is a badass!" said Varun.

"Watch your tongue!Whatif she hears you?What will she think about you?" warned Gaurav.

They finally arrived at the SFU Bureau Headquarter.

SIU Headquarter,

Syria,

After the entering the unit Derifaa introduced the team to their chief, Nabil.

"Chief, theseare the agents from IAT India."

"Welcome to SIU!We will be there for your help till your stayhere. YourChief has already informed us about you all and we have even tracked the name of your link—Saifaz.Further information will be given to you by Agent Derifa and Agent Abbas whowill take over from here", and he asked them to give the information.

Derifa took over,"Right. After your official informed about the man named Saifaz, we tracked him but didn't get anything."

"What about Bilal?" asked Arushi.

"No,nothing.We only got the information about the bank transaction and we tracked it.We only know that there is a transaction taking place every month but we didn't get any name, location or face. And we also found an audio of a call conversation betweenSaifaz and another man."

"Try with the name of Saifaz and see if you can trace anything," suggested Gaurav.

"Why? You only asked us totrack him and now you're asking to track the other name instead—what is this?" frowned Derifa.

"What is this Gaurav?You only found that name now you're telling it is not his name," asked Arushi agitated.

"While I was leaving the room, I got a call from my informer and he told me about that. In fact, that's why I was late byfive minutes and not because I don't have any time-sense," explained Gaurav.

Varunbroke into a smileseeingwhichArushishot him an angry glance, and immediately Varun's face became serious.

"So, what's his real name?" asked Arushi.

"Anybody heard the name Jamal Hussain?" asked Gaurav.

Everyone looked at each other in surprise.

Derifa replied, "Five years ago, he got killed in an attack in Iraq."

"You know these expert terrorists ... they will not get killed easily!So track him down. I, however, doubt if we will get him."

Derifa ordered her subordinates to track and locate him but in their database, they didn't find anything.

"Not only your country, no country in the world will find him," said Gaurav.

"Why?" asked Arushi.

"Because he is like a ghost.No one ever saw his face.When Israel attack happened, did they find his body?" asked Gaurav.

"No, they only found his wallet and ID and as they examine the body they got the information of the deadf body is may be his on one of the dead bodies,"saidDerifa.

"So, think like this—he wasn't killed, he set it up for people to believe that he died in that attack," explained Gaurav.

"Hmm, so we know there will be transaction but we don't know at what time," pointed out Derifa.

"Don't worry, we will handle this. The transaction will take place at the lunch hour of bank,"said Gaurav.

Derifa "Okay, then if you want anything, ask me for whatever you want."

"Is there any restaurant which makes food that's homely?" asked Varun.

"I know of one. I will take you all.Come on, let's go," said Derifa.

At Night,

Derifa's House,

"This restaurant looks like someone's house, agent Derifaa," said

Varun.

"Not 'like' house, it's my house,and don't call me agent call me justDerifa",

"Wow,you place looks very beautiful!" marvelled Arushi.

"Thanks, okay, let get inside."

Derifa's mother greeted them as they entered the house.

"She is my mother," said Diana.

"I was waiting for you for so long!Who are these guests?" asked her mother.

"Maama, these people are from India.They've come here for work. As long as they stay here, we have to take care of them maama," said Derifa.

"Ooh!FromIndia!That is nice; beautiful country, hah!" exclaimed her mother.

"Yes, ma'am, it is beautiful," said Danika.

"Okay,give me some time,I will prepare food",

Arushi and her team asked Derifa,"What makes your mother so happy on hearing our country's name?"

Derifapromptly replied, "Oh, that's because my father is from India,Delhi."

As they were watching the television, Derifa suddenly muted the sound and told Gaurav, "Hey sorry for what I told you at the hotel."

"It's okay!If you don't mind, can I ask a question?" asked Gaurav.

"Yes, sure!"

"What's your mother's name?"

"My mother's name is Aishia."

This is same Aishia who was with Uday the father of Gaurav by hearing the name Gaurav start to think about the Aishia whom he comes know after Srivastav told about his father and Aishia.

On hearing this name,Gaurav remembered once Srivastava had toldhimthat while his father was working undercover, there was an agent he was working together with. Her name was also **Aishia**. Thena thought occurred to him—maybe that **Aishia** and this **Aishia** are both same.

"Err … can I see your father's photo?" asked Gaurav.

Derifa showed her father's photo and said,"This is a very old photo. There are a couple of more photos but not too many."

As soon as he looked at the photo,he was shell-shocked.In that photo, he saw his father,his mother, his sister and himself.

He asked, "Who are these people?"

"They are his first wife and children from that marriage—one is my step-sister and the other is mystep-brother,"Derifa replied.

"Where are they now?" asked Gaurav.

"After the death of my father, I and my mother searched for them but couldn't find them."

Aishia came in to inform,"Food is ready!Comefor dinner."

"Guys, come on!Let's have dinner," saidDerifaa who led them to the dining hall.

Gaurav, however, was still in a state ofshock.Before going for dinner, he called Srivastav.

"What's it? Do you want any information?" asked Srivastava.

"Yes, about the woman**Aishia**,"replied Gaurav.

Srivastava got surprise on hearing that name, "Why?" he asked.

"I think I have found my step-mother and step-sister," said Gaurav.

Both surprised and happy on hearing this, Srivastava asked, "Are you sure it's them?"

"Yes, I am sure.They have my family photo."

"What!Do you want to tell them the truth?" he asked.

Before Gaurav could reply,**Aishia** came into the room and Gaurav quickly added, "Okay,I will talk some other time, good night," and then he abruptly hung up.

"What are you doing here? We all are waiting for you, come on!" said **Aishia**.

While having dinner, Gaurav asked**Aishia**, "While I was looking at the photo, I saw a girl and boy—what about them?"

Aishiabecame silent for a second and then said,"Derifa, I went to look after them after your father passed away. I tried to reach them, but they had already disappeared."

"Then where did they disappear?" askedDerifaa.

"When I went to find them, I got to know that the mother and baby girl had died in a bomb explosion but Icouldn't find the boy," said Aishia.

"Why did you want to search for them?" asked Gaurav.

"Because her father didn't want his children to think negative about him, he loved them very much but couldn't express it to them,"**Aishia** explained.

"Okay, I am sorry," said Gaurav.

Aishiasmiled warmly and said, "It's alright dear, but his last words were,'myboy will come after some yearsand you have to tell them that I loved them both very, very much'. You know, Derifa and I have been waiting for him to come."

"Okay guys, come on, we have to be quick," said Diana.

On hearing all this, Gaurav got emotional.He cried inside.By the time they got done with their dinner, it was too late.

"It is too late today, you all can take rest here," Diana offered.

"No, no ... we'll go to hotel.Why cause problem for you?" said **Aishia**.

"We all have become friends now. What's the problem if you all stay here?In the morning we will go to work from here only," said Diana.

"Can you please get meabedsheet?I don't mind sleeping onthe floor, it's okay," said Varun.

Diana smiled and said,"Okay, I will get one," and took them to different rooms. She also was going to sleep when she saw Gaurav staring at the photo of her and her mother.

"It is cute,isn't it?" she asked.

"No, it's beautiful, because you have a family," he replied.

"Why?Youdon't have any?" she asked.

"When I was little, my parents and sister died in an accident.You know, I also had a sister like you," he answered.

Diana felt sad and sorry for Gaurav as she went to sleep.

Next Day,

SIU Unit,

Everyone reportedat the SIU unit asChief Nabil called them and told about the transaction.

"Okayagents, three of our agents will go undercover at the bank and we will track them on camera so you guys be at the unit until we get them here," said Chief Nabil.

"Sir, we will also come," said Arushi.

"No, this is my country and my rules, so listen to me," said Chief Nabil strictly.

"Okay then, kindly lead the mission," said Abhiram.

"Let's do it!" cried Chief Nabil.

"Guys, believe me, we will catch him," said Diana.

"Okay guys, let them handle this," said Arushi.

"That's fine. Moreover, we have some work to do," said Gaurav.

"Alright then, I will be in touch," said Diana and then left with her teamfor the bank.

Gaurav and Varun, meanwhile, began to track them.

Local Bank, Syria

At Lunch Hour,

At the bank, exactly at the lunch hour, the jeep stopped in front of the bank.All the SFU agents were ready.Two men came out of the jeep.Seeingthat,Dianaordered,"Agents, are you ready? Take the four guards out and take the two men who were wearing suits with them in custody". After she gave the order, the agents took the guards by sniper and they used silencer for not hear the voice of shot and two men were in custody after taking them in custody they were blindfolded and took them in to their safe house.While seeing this Arushi and her team got happy for getting the man.

SIUSafe House:

The SFU agents and the two men were in the safe house when Diana called Arushi,

"Guys, you can come now. I will send you the car from the safe house."

"Thanks, Diana," said Arushi.

Once the IAT agents reached the safe house, Diana said, "Agents, we have them in custody.Whatever interrogation is required, you will do ithere.Antinois a specialist in interrogation so he will be a help for you."

Arushithanked Diana and also ordered Abhiram to go and join Antino in interrogating them because he too is a specialist in interrogation.

The two men were taken to the interrogation room and Antino uncovered their faces and introduced the Agents. Gaurav entered the interrogation room, took the cell fromAntinotocheck the number.Hethen dialed the number which he had had, and the mobile rang inSaifaz's coat pocket.Antino took it out from the pocket and showed it to Gaurav. As soon as Gaurav looked at the number, he got shocked because the number displaying was the same number which was used to transfer the money.

"It's the same number," Gaurav said to his team.

"That means we have hunted down the right prey," Antino replied to Gaurav.

Some other officersthen entered the room and grabbedSaifaz to the nextroom to interrogate him.

"Who are you?" asked Antino to Saifaz.

"I am a normal person," Saifaz replied.

"Whomareyou working for?" Antino asked.

"I am not working with anyone, I am just a normal man who comes to the bank to withdraw money," Saifaz replied nonchalantly.

"And what do you know about Mohammad?"

"I don't know any Mohammad."

"What was the money for—that you withdrew a while ago?"

"I don't know anything about that and about any money transaction."

As, the interrogation continued, Gaurav got bored and tried to walk out. He had a feeling that this was futile.The man didn't seemto give outanything.

"I will be waiting outside the room," Gaurav said to Arushi.

"Wait for a bit," Arushi said.

"I am hearing this for an hour," Gaurav drawled and then he left the room.as after few minutes later Gaurav looks at the room where bodyguard locked up and Gaurav asks for food to Harleen and she looks at Arushi and arushi nodes her head to give what he ask. And then Harleen orders the food to his soldier to bring and the soldier told as she told and brings the food and gives it to Gaurav.

After several attempts, when nothing came out of that interrogation, Gaurav asked Arushi, "Can I try?"

"But you're not a field agent or an interrogator! Can you do it?"Arushi asked sceptically.

"Trust me," Gaurav said and having Arushi's approval, he went into the interrogation room.

Gaurav took the food and entered the room. He kept the plate infront of the bodyguard and asked himto eat, but the bodyguard hesitated. He was afraid of the food being poisoned.

"It is not poisoned.Eat," said Gaurav gently.

But even then the bodyguard didn't touch the plate. So, Gaurav exchanged the plates.The bodyguard finally began to eat as he was starving.

"so, you understood while back there about the money transaction," Gaurav asks to Bodyguard

As silent for second

"So, you do this often … kidnapping innocent people and capture them and interrogate them?" asked the bodyguard.

"You're my first actually.How am I doing?" Gaurav smiled and then added,"I am an Analyst."

"What does that mean?" Bodyguard asked.

"That means, I work behind the desk," Gaurav answered, to which the bodyguard nodded.

"So, now you tell me, what do you do?" Gaurav asked.

"I am a bodyguard," Bodyguard shrugged.

There was a brief pause when Gaurav's eyes examined the man's calloused and scarred hands. With his eyes fixed on those marks, Gaurav asked, "How did you get those scars?"

Bodyguard looked at his hands and replied, "These scars are from my childhood … when I was a boy."

Meanwhile, outside the safe house, 3 to 4 cars stopped and groups of terrorists got down in a rush. They began to surround the entire place.

"How do you know Saifaz," asked Gaurav, inside the interrogation room.

"I am his bodyguard."

"How do you know him?"

"He is my boss and I really don't talk tohim much."

"But you hear what he is talking about; did you hear the name of Mohammad?"

"I don't know anything about his work."

"Tell me about your family," probed Gaurav.

"I have a wife and two kids, I don't think I will see them ever again."

"If you cooperate with us, we can promise you that you will see your family again and nothing will happen to them."

"But I don't think you willgettosee your family again," said the bodyguard, as a smile appeared on his face.

"Why? What does that mean?" asked Gaurav.

All of a sudden, they all heard explosions outside. Gaurav turned to look at the bodyguard's face.

"What's happening Diana?" asked Gaurav.

"We have been attacked," Diana replied through the microphone.

Gaurav looked at the bodyguard with rage and asked, "What is this?Are these are your people?"

"You were right all the while. I am Saifaz," said the bodyguard, andthen, suddenly, they were interrupted by the terrorists.They heard the sound of explosions and firing of guns.They all got ready with their own arms and reloaded them.Everybody took out their guns and reloaded them.As they headed out of the room, a terrorist seemed to be approaching at the door.The agents immediately covered behind the wall but within those few seconds of movements, some of the agents got hit by bullets. The others began to backfire without further ado.The firing continued up to five more minutes and then a man came out and threw agrenadeinto the room.Within seconds the room exploded and parts of the building collapsed. Arushi and Diana, buried beneath the debris, were trying to push the chunks of concrete above them when two terrorists attacked them.They grabbed their neck from behind, giving a tight pull which tore their muscles. One more terrorist was about to attack the girls from behind when Varun quickly took him down with a gun. Hearing the commotion, more terroristsran to the room. Abhiram and Antino startedfiring at them all.

"Alright, Varun and Danika, youguyscover us while I and Diana will go get Gaurav and that bodyguard," instructed Arushi.

Varun and Danika agreed to cover them.Arushi and Diana went to the interrogation room but the room had already collapsed and they couldn't see Gaurav or thebodyguard.They started to scream Gaurav's name and finally a hand came up from under the debris of stones.Theyknew that was Gaurav so both of them went to grab him.They also tried to pull up the bodyguard but he was not in conscious so Gaurav tookthe weight of his bodyon his shoulder.But more terroristsstarted to come in and fire at them.Arushithengave a gun to Gaurav and said, "Do you know how to use this thing?"

"Why?He doesn't know?" asked Diana incredulously.

"He is not a field agent. I think this is his first field job," replied Arushi.

"Guys, I have also served in thearmy; I know how to use things," said Gaurav andthen Gaurav suddenly remembered the bodyguard who had just claimed to be Saifaz.

"Oh no!" criedAntino and Abhiram when they heard it from Gaurav.

Varun had been covering for them while they were shooting at them, and Gaurav tookthe bodyguardwho was resting on his shoulder and started walking.They were on their way when another explosion took place, followed by a dead silence. Many agents lay dead, while some got up. The agents walked towards the interrogation room where Saifaz was supposed to stay but nobody except Abhiram and Antino were in the room.They tried to wake the unconscious agents butAntinodidn't wake up. He was dead.Abhiramregained consciousness, but, in pain, he said in a quivering voice, "They've gotSaifaz."

"What!Oh no!" gasped Arushi.

Diana, meanwhile, was still in shock on seeing her partner dead. Gaurav looked at her mournful face. After a short while, the SFU medical team came to pick them up and take them to their unit for treatment.

SIU Unit,

Diana and the IAT Agents finally recovered from the injuries from the attack. The other man with Saifaz, who was the real bodyguard, wasn't dead but had gotten severely injured and had gone into a comatose state.With the full support from the Syrian government,Arushi and Gaurav and their team were taking the bodyguard into their custody and were flying him to India.

"Guys, it was nice to see you!We will meet again soon," said Diana.

"Yes!It was good working with you.Thank you very much for all the help," said Arushi.

"It was our duty," said Diana.

"And … really sorry about you partner," apologized Arushi.

The moment Antino got mentioned, Diana got emotional. She also remembered about Gaurav losing his family.Shewent near him said, "Gaurav,don't feel bad about family, we all are here for you."

As soon as she said this, he got emotional and hugged her.Theyall were surprised.

"Alright Agents, your government is ready for you at the airport.So, come on!" said Chief Nabil.

As they were on their way to the airport their cars suddenly came to a halt. It was soon followed by heavy firing. They had again been attacked by terrorists who had come in a van. They scurried to hideouts and then began to throwgranitesatthem.Arushi, Varun, Danika and Abhiramdidn't stop shooting at them but a sudden bomb explosionnear Diana's jeep shocked them.Onseeing that, Gaurav was enraged as he had only foundhissister after years!If anything happened to her,he would lose that one chance in having a family.Whilemost of the agents in her van died, Diana remained stuck in the car, alive.

She talked into the walkie-talkie, "Arushi, take your guys and the captive and go.I will manage this lot."

"Noway!We can't leave you like this!" revolted Arushi.

"This is not about me,this is about our countries, so please take them all and go to the airport which is the other way," commanded Diana.

Even after constant firing by Diana and the agents, it wasn't useful. The terrorists started to surround them.

Arushi all of a sudden noticed something and said, "Where is Gaurav?"

Almost immediately she and her team heard a bike's noise.They turned around and saw Gaurav riding towards them in a bike.He grabbed the guns from Arushi and started to fire at the terrorists. He then wentto rescue Diana from the car, which after they are attacked had exploded and caught flames.However, the bodyguard could not be saved. He died before he could be rescued.

Local Hospital,

Syria,

All of them were admitted to the hospital because of the attack— Abhiram's leg had fractured and Diana got shot. Gaurav fractured his back and also got shot on his leg. Diana's mother had rushed to see her daughter at the hospital.

"Diana!Oh my baby!How are you?" cried Aishia.

"Mum, why have you come here? I am fine!It's just a small wound, that's it!If Gaurav had notrescuedme,I would have been dead." Diana explained.

"Shh! Don't you say that! Oh! but where is he?" she asked, looking for Gaurav.

"He just went outside."

"Okay, I will come back in minute," said Aishia and went outside to seeGaurav.After a second of searching, he came in front of her.She looked at him in awe and gratitude with tears brimming her eyes as she hugged him.

"Hey, ma'am, nothing has happened to your daughter ... your daughter is a fighter, she never gives up!" he comforted her.

"I know that.She is like her father," said Aishia.

Gaurav instantly got emotional on hearing his father's name and asked,"Washer father a great man?"

"Oh yeah!He was a great man, and he also loved the family very much, took care of them just like you did today," she smiled warmly.

"No, ma'am, that was my duty," said Gaurav.

"Duty or love?" asked Aishia.

"What are you saying ma'am? Ilookather like a sister!" said Gaurav.

Aishiaimmediately replied, "I know that, Gaurav, I also know where you were yesterday at night.You came to my room where I and Diana were sleeping. I saw you taking the photo of your parents and sisters aswell as ours. I know you are his son,"Aishia finished.

"N-no, ma'am!What are you talking about?" Gaurav stammered.

"I know, I seeitin your eyes," said Aishia.

After a pause, Gaurav said, "How did you findout?"

"When you came to our house yesterday, I noticed you have the same birthmark likeUday's son had.But then I got confused—name and mark all are same—but Istilldidn't agree that you are my son. But while having dinner, when I asked you about your family, I saw it in your eyes, through your silenttears."

Gaurav remained silent for a few seconds and then hugged her tightly, and asked,"Can I call you mom?"

Aishiasmiled as she got emotional and hugged him. She said,"You two are myonlyfamily I am leftwith!Okaycome,I will talk to Diana. She will be very happy, you know!Ever since she was achildshewould ask about yousaying,'ifmy brother is there, then he will be grown up and someday come to see me!' She always talks about you!Come on!"

"Mom, no, I don't want to be in her life. I am happy and satisfied by seeing both of you.This is fine with me," said Gaurav.

"Why?"

"I already have one sister who doesn't love mebutonly hates me," said Gaurav painfully.

"Well, Diana loves you very much and she waits to see you,Gaurav,since a long time."

"What if she doesn't like me and hates me?ThenIwon't be left with anything ... I don't want to barge into her life. Let her be happy like this. I just want to see her like this.You don't worry. I don't know if shewill be happy if I stay in her life, so, I don't want to hurt her."

Aishia was touched by what Gaurav said.She sensed his innocence and brotherly love for his sisterDaina.

"Don't cry now,Iwill come to see you," said Gaurav.

"Please be with us," pleaded Aishia.

"Don't worry, if I feellikeseeing you both, I will come here and if you want see me, just call me and I will be here, mother!"

"I am very happy to see you," said **Aishia**.

Then Diana called out from inside, "Mom, where are you?"

They both went inside the room where Arushi, Abhiram and Diana were taking rest.

Dianasaid, "sorry, brother, my mom is sentimental.Don't feel bad."As soon as she saw her mother in the eye, Diana knew that her mother had been cryinginfront of Gaurav.

On hearing the word brother from her mouth, he was overjoyed and Aishia too got very happy.

"Sorry, can I call you my brother?Youknow,I had a brother but Inever sawhim.He's probably of your age," said Diana.

Aishia got emotional and looked at Gaurav who replied, "It will be my pleasure! I am happy."

After sometime,Aishia and Gaurav went outside and **Aishia** said, "Please don't forget about us!"

"No, mother!Iwill be in touch with you and please don't tellherabout me," he reminded.

They all had some hours torelax together and havesomefun before they got ready to return to the India.

"By the way, I'm sorry about the bodyguard … I know he was the only link you had got,' said Diana remorsefully.

"It's okay. Gaurav will look for something else," said Arushi.

"If you need any help, I will be here," said Diana.

"Okay, thanks!" said Arushi.

"**Brother …** please don't forget about me…"added Diana.

"I will not.You are like my sister, why would I forget about you?See you soon," smiled Gaurav.

"I will be in touch," said Diana.

They all said their goodbyes and then the flight took off from Syria.

Tehran,

Iran,

After what happened yesterday to her children,Madiha got scared and thought, "If I stay with my children here, we will not be safe.I have to get out of here quickly!"That very evening, she got a call from the Visa office,

"Madam, is thisMadiha?"

"Yes, speaking."

"We are from thevisa office.You had applied for your visa, along with your children'sfor India."

"Yes madam."

"Madam, you have to come and talk to our superior."

"Why madam?Is there a problem?"

"No, madam.It is the rule for anybody applying for visa.They have to come to our office and speak to our superior."

"Is this compulsory?"

"Yes madam, otherwise your visa might be rejected."

"Okay madam, I will come."

After they disconnected the call, she started to think how she would get out ofthere.She keptthinking about her children and herself. But, unfortunately, that call was also heard by Abdul Rana who got extremely surprised and shocked.

Chapter 5
YET ANOTHER ATTACK

After that attack in Syria, they lost the only one answer to what would happen—where it will happen—or who is behind all this. Now once again they were back to square one.They didn't even know what their next plan would be, so now they have to find some other clue otherwise their country would not be safe. After the attack,Abhiram was badly injured, so he was admitted to the hospital and Gaurav had fractured his hand and back.

Delhi, India

RAW,

After landing, the RAW called a meeting to discuss about what hadhappened.So, all the units had gathered once again for a meeting.

"Kulkarni, I believe in you, but what your people have done is just nothing," said the RAW Chief.

"Sir, we didn't know that was coming," replied Kulkarni.

The RAW Chief replied, "If you can't save one person, how will you save the country?"

"I know we made a big mistake, sir, but we will get you an answer," said Kulkarni.

The SFU Chief spoke up, "No, sir!This is not a game.This is about our country's security sir!"

"Yes, SFU Chief is right," said the RAW Chief.

"Sir, we will surely do something!" defended Chief Kulkarni.

"No, we will not take any chance, Kulkarni. I will give to somebody else now. Time is running out and yetyou did nothing significant," said RAW Chief indignantly.

"Sir, please. our team tried really hard.Please don't take this missionawayfrom us," pleaded Kulkarni.

The RAW Chief replied, "I know you have got talented agents and technicians but we arerunning out of time so you have to do something NOW!" After apause,the RAW Chief decided,"Okay, now onwards, SFU will handle it and IAT will work under the SFU unit.So, Shrikant Talwar will be control of this mission and Kulkarni you will be under him.Whateverinformation you have, pleasebrief him and work like a team. Shrikant, best of luck!"

Absolutely elated, Shrikant wasthrilledtolead thismission.He threw Kulkarni a quick glance andhis lips curved into a cunning smile.

"Thank you, sir! I will do my best and give you a report," said Shrikant.

After the meeting, Shrikant asked Kulkarni to wait for him at the lobby. Kulkarni kept waiting for nearly 20–30 minutes and after a while Shrikant came with his agent,Harleen. Shewas a special agent in the SFU unit.

Shrikantwent to Kulkarni and said,"Hey, Kulkarni, bring all the files and information about this mission and also ask your teamtocome. We'll meet youallat our unit," said Shrikant.

They left the RAW Headquarter. Kulkarni was bad upset but was left with no choice.He was bound by his duty and orders from his seniors.

Hospital,

As after the landing in India, the IAT team was transferred to the hospital for treatment.Abhiramhad the worst injury while Gaurav was better,andArushi, Varun and Danika got small injuries.

Kulkarni went to see his team at the hospital and also tell them that the mission was no longer in their hands.

'So, guys, how are you?" asked Kulkarni.

They all said they were fine and just when they asked Kulkarni about him, the doctor entered in the ward where they admitted. On seeing Gaurav, the doctor said,"Hey!Are you Sakshi's brother?"

"Yes! Why?" asked Gaurav, slightly taken aback.

"I guessed so! I saw you at your bakery that day," said the doctor.

"Oh! I didn't notice, sorry," said Gaurav politely.

"It's okay."

"What is your name?" asked Gaurav.

"IamIndu! Your sister's best friend.We work together in this hospital."

I guessed so! I saw you at your bakery that day," said the doctor.

I didn't notice, sorry," said Gaurav politely.

's okay."

What is your name?" asked Gaurav.

amIndu! Your sister's best friend.We work together in this hospital."

Gaurav began to introduce his team one by one,Indu interruptedandsaid,"OhI know all your names! I saw all of you that day," and then she started to name each one.They all laughed about it.

I don't quite recognize this manthough.Who is he?"Indu asked.

orry! He is our boss, Chief Kulkarni," said Gaurav.

What's the work you all do?And how did this accident happen?"

e do business of raw materials for factor

"

"

h, okay!"

Kulkarni interrupted Induandasked,"

when can they start to workagain?Are they fit enough?"

hat are you saying sir?!They didn't get minor injuries!" said Indu disbelievingly. She show him the files of Abhiram and said,"e broke his leg and he can't even stand properly

As Gaurav began to introduce his team one by one,Indu interruptedandsaid,"OhI know all your names! I saw all of you that day," and then she started to name each one.They all laughed about it.

"I'm sorry, I don't quite recognize this manthough.Who is he?"Indu asked.

"Sorry! He is our boss, Chief Kulkarni," said Gaurav.

"Ah great!What's the work you all do?And how did this accident happen?"

They all exchanged quick glances and Gaurav said, "We do business of raw materials for factories."

"Oh, okay!"

Kulkarni then interrupted Induandasked,"DrIndu, when can they start to workagain?Are they fit enough?"

"What are you saying sir?!They didn't get minor injuries!" said Indu disbelievingly. She went on to show him the files of Abhiram and said,"He broke his leg and he can't even stand properly.At least not forayear!Hecan'twalk."

Then she flipped through Gaurav's files and said,"His hand mightget fixedin 12 days but I can't tell."

"What do you mean by 'I can't tell'?" asked Kulkarni, alarmed.

"His back was hit by a very heavy object so if he does anything crazier, it can't be cured," said Indu.

"I Can't stay like that for my whole life! I have to get to work!"

groaned Abhiram.

"Okay, I understand … but you can't even stand! So, I think you will have to take care of yourself",

After sometime, Kulkarni called Arushi outside and said,"You know we have got a bigger problem, so, I want you to bring all of your team except Abhiram to the safe house."

"Right. But why not Abhiram, sir?"

"I saw his health report just now. He has got a lot of damage and he is our one of the best agents, so I don't want to lose him.He has to take rest. Inform the others to meet me at the safe house sharp at 11:00AM. Gaurav will give the location but don't bring Gaurav, he also has to take rest. His condition doesn't seem fit enough."

After that, Kulkarni went to the unit and Arushi went to the ward. The visiting time was over, so they bade goodbye to their families.

"I have some work so I have to go now.You take the children and go home. I will return late at night,"Arushi said to her husband, who nodded and left the hospital with their children.

Once the room was empty, Gaurav asked Arushi, "What happened and why did the chief call you outside and what did he tell you?"

Arushireplied, "Sir has asked me to go to the safe house with the others."

"Okay then, let's go," said Gaurav.

"No, no, not you!Only the three of us,"said Arushi as she gestured towards Varun and Danika.

"If you want the location of the safe house, you have to let me in," said Gaurav.

"No.You and Abhiram got to take rest.It's an order from sir."

"I can't follow this order.Let's not waste time.Come on, let's go!"

"But, we have to follow the hospital rules"Arushi replied.

"No, I can't," replied Gaurav.

"You have to listen to your boss, I am commanding!" exclaimed Arushi.

Finally, Gaurav agreed to her boss Arushi, and Dr Inducame in and took Gaurav to theX-rayroom. As they entered theX-ray room,Indu scanned his leg and told Gaurav that she will send the reports through mobile. And everybody left the hospital straight towards the unit.

Gaurav's Safe House

They all went straight to the safe house exactly at 11:00AM, Including Srivastava.

"I asked you not to bring Gaurav," Kulkarni said, looking grimly at Arushi.

Arushiexplained, "But sir, you know that he will not listen to even you in this case.He surely wouldn't listen to me!"

"Fine!Now that we all are here, we can start," said Kulkarni.

"Why did you call me? Whatwasso urgent that all we had to meetat the safe house?" asked Srivastava looking at Kulkarni.

Everybody asked the same thing.

"Alright, guys, after the failed mission in Syria, RAW is not happy with us."

"Why sir?Wewere the ones to find about the attack, sir, and we had come so close to the mission!" revolted Varun.

"I know that, but the RAW is not taking any chance this time."

"What do you mean by 'not taking any chance'?" asked Danika.

After hearing the chief, Gaurav said, "It means that they have thrown our team out of this mission."

"Gaurav, how did you know that?" asked Kulkarni.

"I knew it from the beginning," said Gaurav.

"How can they just take our mission like this?Our team has battled death and ...Abhiram is at the hospital for this mission!Now they are excluding usfrom this mission?" said Arushi furiously.

"The order is from the RAW. I can't do anything," said Kulkarni.

"Then who is leading the mission?" asked Srivastava.

"SFU unit chief, Srikant, and his agent Harleen."

"I knew he wasn't happy with us right from the start. Never liked that we were leading the mission.Sohe just chanced upon this opportunity," said Gaurav.

"What about us?We have to keep quiet after all this work?" asked Varun.

"No. RAW gave the order that from now onwards IAT will work under SFU," informed Kulkarni.

"What?No way, sir!" exclaimed Arushi.

"This can't behappening.Isthis a dream or is this real?" shivered Danika.

They all started to raise their voices in revolt against this unjust decision by RAW.

Kulkarni interrupted them, "Okay guys, cool … calm down … we don't have any choice, we have to give the all information to them tomorrow. Varun and Danika will work for them and deliver information to them," Kulkarni said with a note of finality.

"Sir, what are you saying, sir? W-we can't do this…" trailed off Arushi.

"Arushi, we don't have any choice, so, pleasecooperate.If we have to succeedinthis mission and keep our country safe, then we have to do this," said Kulkarni.

Even thoughtheyall finally agreed, their faces were small.Theywere not comfortable with this decision.They left for their houses but Gaurav asked Srivastava to stay back in the safe house for a minute.

"What is this about?" asked Srivastava.

"Remember you had told me in childhood that when my father was an undercover agent in Syria, he had married a woman named Madiha and lived there?"

"Yeah, that is true now.But what does that have to do with this or anything else?" Srivastava looked puzzled.

"I met them in Syria … I met my mother and I have a sister too," said Gaurav.

"What are you saying?"

"Yes, and she works for the Syrian government just like I do for India," said Gaurav and went on to show him their picture.

"Yes, she was married to your father!Did you meet your sister?"

"I met both, mother and sister, and mother was very happy on seeing me.She, in fact, recognized me and thought of telling Diana that I am her brother. But I strictly asked her not to."

"But why?"

"I remembered how Sakshi hates me. What if I told Diana about me and then she also wouldn't like me?I can't take so much!"

"Hey fool!She is your blood relation. Of courseshe will be happy to see you! Sakshi is not your real sister that way."

"No,Sakshiisa sister to me from my childhood.Both are my sisters and I can't lose them!"

"So, how do you feel after meeting your family?" asked Srivastava, smiling. Gaurav smiled back to him, just enough to show how happy he was.

After that, the two of them went for dinner.

Srivastava'sCafe

While Gaurav and Srivastava were having dinner together, Sakshi arrived at the bakery to pick up her father.Then she saw Gaurav and got very angry.

"Dad, I thought you're busy at work, but it is not that!I see you're enjoying your time with him. Whereas mother and I have been waiting for you for dinner!"

"Oh no!I didn't know about that … I'm so sorry for this," apologized Gaurav.

"Because of you, my parents got separated and now once again it is happening!" she snapped.

"Sakshi, what are you saying?He is your brother and you have to accept it!"scowled Srivastava.

"No, he is not my brother and, once again, I am ordering you to stay out of my family!" she said turning at Gaurav and then looked at her father and said,"Dad, you want him or me? Decide."

"What are you saying, Sakshi?You both are my children. I don't have to choose between you both, so stop acting like a child!" scolded Srivastava.

"No, you have to decide between me and him because I can't see you and mum separate once again, so…"

Feeling guilty, Gaurav said,"Okay, okay, I will stay out of all your lives. I will not see you again."

"Don't you come near to me and my family till you live," scowled Sakshi.

"What are you saying, Gaurav? I gave a word to your mother," said Srivastava.

"Right now, my mother's word is not as important as your family," said Gaurav and turning to Sakshi he said,"Iam sorry, Sakshi, for all that I done to you."

Gaurav got up from the table and left quietly, leaving a very sad Srivastava behind.

Gaurav's House,

After all of that happened, he went to his house, constantly thinking about whatjust happened at the cafe. He took a look at the photo of Aishia and **Diana** that he had brought back with him and felt slightly better,lighter;his face broke into a faint smile which kept him going through the night.

Hospital,

Next morning at the hospital, all of them went to meet Abhiram and told him all about RAW's order.

Feeling horrible, Abhiram said, "I want to join now!"

"No, now it's time to take rest.For yourself and your family," said Arushi.

"Arushiiscorrect.You have to stay here and take a rest.And Gaurav, I had told you to stay back for scanning of your back yesterday, but you just left.So now can we go for it," said Indu.

"SorryIndu! I have an important work now. But I will surely come for that in the evening."

"No, you have to take rest!Can I call your boss and talk to him about this?"

"No, please!This is very important, so I will meet you in evening," and before Indu could say anything else, they all left the hospital in hurry.

IndulookedatAbhiram and asked, "Is he always like that?"

Abhiramreplied, "Yes, he is always like that.He will not listen to anybody but him. However, don't worry.He sticks to his words. He'll come by evening."

"Alright!You take rest. Let me know whenever you want anything. I will be here, so ask me."

Abhiram's wife arrived to visit him and Indu left the room to give the family some privacy.

SFU Unit,

After RAW had given the order to IAT to work under SFU, all IAT staff shifted to the SFU unit, including Kulkarni and his team, except Abhiram because he was still admitted at the hospital.

"Where is your team?" asked Shrikant.

"They are coming.They will be here in 5 minutes," replied Kulkarni.

IAT team just reached when Shrikant said, "Your team doesn't have any time sense at all!How will we work together like this?That's why you all failed in the mission," grunted Shrikant in front of all of them. They all got angry. Shrikant said,"Okay, whatever you have got, please hand it over to us."

"And what about us?" asked Kulkarni.

"Whenever we will need for your help, we will ask you.Untilthen, just follows our lead."

"No! that's not—" Varun began to speak but was cut short byShrikant, "If anybody tells me what to do, I will suspend them."

"Right, it's okay with us.Now can you show us the chamber wherewe'llbe working," said Kulkarni.

Srikant told Harleen to show them their chambers, and she took them to their chambers.

On their way, Harleen said, "I was told that IAT has never failed a single mission;Ireckon that was not true,eh?"

"Wehaven't failed, we are just one step behind," retorted Arushi.

After IAT had settled in their new chamber, Shrikant came in and said,"I want all the files and information about this mission as well as any evidencefoundin Syria."

"Right," said Arushi.

"Didn't your chiefteach you how to respect your superiors?" asked Shrikant.

"Sorry, sir," said Arushi.

"Harleen, take Varun and Danika with you andget a brief on any evidence from Syria," ordered Shrikant.

Harleen said, "Yes, sir!"

Once they all had left the chamber,Gaurav looked at Kulkarni and said, "Chief, I think I know what this is all about."

"What?How did you know?"

"After the first attack that had happened in the Syria, that bodyguard had given me some clues,Chief," whispered Gaurav.

"What are those?" asked Kulkarni.

"He told me about SCIMITAR," said Gaurav and began to take stuff out from his bag. He scanned them to look for evidence and then suddenly they found a code:'5.13.2.1.19.19.25 The Great King Bharat'"

"What are those?" asked Arushi curiously.

"Maybe it's a code for something or maybe a location," guessed Kulkarni.

"No, sir, after decoding I have found thatitsays'EMBASSY'," informed Gaurav.

"Then what is GAUL?" asked Arushi.

"After researching all the information, I learnt that GAUL is the old name of France," Gaurav said.

"Does that mean that the next attack will at the France embassy?" asked Arushi.

Gaurav replied, "I think so."

"Why didn't you tell this earlier?" asked Kulkarni.

Gaurav replied, "I don't believetheSFU Chief Shrikant."

"Sir, please give us more clarity. Gauravhas been lying to us right from the start,"Arushi bit her lips.

Kulkarni was taken aback, "Why? What happened?What did he lie about?"

"You told us that he is not a field agent and he is an analyst, but in Syria, while we were attacked by terrorist group, he fought like he was trained or maybe he served for the country",

"Ohthat!" Kulkarni heaved a sigh of relief.

"Gaurav, if you want us to work like a team and like friends, then you have to tell us everything about you," said Arushi.

"Yes, that's true, Gaurav, you have to tell them the truth," Kulkarni said.

Gaurav thought for a while and said, "Yes, I was trained and I served for the country. I was a soldier."

"Then why were you suspended?"

"I can't say more! I will not."

"You must!" insisted Arushi.

"It is personal, so, sorry."

Kulkarni interrupted, "Why aren't you telling them the truth?"

Arushi looked at them quizzically and asked, "Why, what happened?"

Kulkarni spoke up, "He was suspended because he left my sonamongsta terrorist group."

Gaurav got angry and cried, "No!Youvery well know that I didn't leave him behind! He was like a brother to me!Whywould I want that?"

"Well, that is true,"said Kulkarni.

"Okay guys, I am sorry. I was the one who brought this matter up. So, let's move on to this mission," said Arushi.

"Okay then, what else have you got?" asked Kulkarni.

Gaurav began, "The man who toldus that he was just a bodyguard was Saifaz himself."

"What?" asked a shocked Kulkarni.

"Yes, sir, after the attack, the bodies were taken to the forensic department and I gave a call to the doctor and he gave me this information," said Gaurav.

"So,the man who called himselfSaifaz—who was he?" asked Kulkarni.

"We do not understand sir," said Gaurav.

"Is anything else that you know?" asked Kulkarni.

"I got an information from my informer that they have a mission named'*SCIMITAR*'."

Kulkarnisaid,"That means we have to inform the RAW immediately," and then he dashed to Shrikant's chamber and informed all of this and also called the RAW Chief to deliver the information."

On hearing the whole thing, RAW called for a meeting.

RAW Headquarter,

At the meeting, all the units gathered as the RAW chief asked Srikant about the mission.

Shrikant replied, "Sir, we are very close to succeeding in the mission and we have got all the information about the next attack as well!"

RAW Chief asked interestedly, "So, go on!Tell us everything!"

Shrikant then went on to show the video of the interrogation from Syria where Kulkarni's team had interrogated the two men.

RAW Chief said, "He is telling that he is Saifaz!What's that?"

"No, sir, he is not the man.Seethebodyguard?He is the real Saifaz," replied Shrikant.

"Then who is that man?" asked the RAW Chief.

Srikant answered, "We don't know about him,sir.We are tracking him but we aren't able to find any information about him yet."

The RAW Chief asked, "So, what's next?"

Then Srikant showed him the code.

RAW Chief asked, "What's this code?"

Srikant promptly replied, "Sir, my team has cracked itanddecoded EMBASSY Gaul."

"That means the Indian Embassy in Parisis the next target!" exclaimed the RAW Chief.

"But we don't understand … why France?" asked Chief Kulkarni.

Afterbeingsilent for a few minutes,theRAWChief suddenly realizedsomething. "There is a meeting in France with our prime minister."

"So … they are planning a bigger attack," said Kulkarni.

Srikant added, "Yes, sir, I believe their mission's name is SCIMITAR."

RAW Chief ordered, "Right then, get your team ready and I will talk to the PM have a word with the French authority and I will update you. Meanwhile, find more information about the SCIMITAR."

"Okay,sir," replied Shrikant.

After the meeting, Kulkarni and his team felt bad because all the hard work was done by them but all the credits were given to the SFU unit and Shrikant's team.

Kulkarni told his team,"Okay, try to dig deeper; we will get something else."

Theteam agreed and then left for the hospital to see Abhiram.

Hospital,

At Night,

Then all were in Abhiram'scabin, talking and laughing.They told him all about the mission and then DrIndu came tocheckAbhiram,"How are you feeling?"

"I am feeling well, and Gaurav will be here to take care of me," replied Abhiram.

Gaurav immediately threw Abhiram a scornful look.

"Okay Gaurav, come on!We have to take a quick scan so that we know how you actually are right now," said Indu.

Gaurav sighed and replied, "Okay doctor, let's go!"

Arushi, Varun and Danikagot up to leave and said,"Guys, we will meet tomorrow. Take care and good night guys!"

Abhiramsaid, "Yeah good night.Thanks for coming here!"

Indu took Gaurav to the X-ray room and asked him to lie on the bed. She began to scan his whole body. Gaurav suddenly asked,"Doctor, are you free tonight?"

Indu casually replied, "Yes, after this I am free.Butwhy would you ask that?"

After a brief pause, Gaurav asked, "Can we go for dinner tonight?" he gulped.

Indu looked at Gaurav, "Are you asking me for a date?"

Gaurav quickly replied, "N-no!Not like a date ...ju-just as friends..."

Indu smiled and replied, "Alright!I will join you."

The scanning was completed when Indu said, "We're done here. Wait for a minute, I will back."

"Okay, I will be in Abhiram's room."

"Okay!"

When Indu was done wrapping up, she went inside Abhiram's room, "Gaurav?Can we go now?"

"Yup!Let'sgo!Abhi, take rest and good night."

"Good night!"saidAbhiramand winked while Gaurav thanked him and they both went for dinner.

Once they were settled in the restaurant,Indu asked Gaurav about his family.

Gaurav replied, "I don't know much about them but I do know that my father was a great man and my mother loved me very much."

"I know Sakshi; why is she so angry with you all the time? I didn't ask her about this before but I am actually curious," said Indu.

"After my parents died, her father took care of me and took me to his house but her mother didn't like that. So, for small misunderstanding, they got separated."

"So, that's why she is very angry with you!But you love her very much..."

Gaurav replied, "Ya ... I love her very much. I can do anything for her because they are all I have left."

Indu consoled him, "Don't worry, someday she will understand you ... until then, I will be there for you..."

As they finished theirdinner,Indusaid,"I had a good time with you, thanks for inviting!"

"And thank you for joining me," smiled Gaurav.

After that, they both greeted each other good night and left the restaurant.

Gaurav's House,

After coming back home fromdinner,Gaurav started to work on the mission and searched for any information he couldfind.After a sometime of searching all the files in his system, he saw a file inside the folder "CLASSIFIED".He got doubtful and out of curiosity, he opened the file.But since the file wasclassified,it could only be opened by superiors, so the file didn't open. All through the night he made several attempts, but all in vain!

Next Morning,

SFU Unit,

Kulkarni called his teammates to the SFU unit for some urgent work, so everybody headed quickly.

Arushi entered and asked, "I got your message, Sir!What is so urgent?"

Kulkarni replied, "After Gaurav gave us the clue about the next attack, the RAW chief clarified it further and it is true!There will be an attack at theIndian Embassy in Paris three weeks from now. There have been some suspicious movements there and after all the local authorities followed up, they found weapons.So, RAW asked our PM's permission to go to France. The PM has accepted."

"I think we were not allowed to go on a mission," said Varun.

Kulkarni said, "No, we are going!"

Danika said, "What sir? Did RAW give us the permission?"

"No, SFU is still leading this mission.So, under their lead agent,Harleen and top agents of SFU and four agents from IAT will be going to France,"informed Chief Kulkarni.

"I don't think this is a good idea sir," protested Arushi.

"I think we don't have a choice. If we want be a part of the mission, we have to join hands with SFU," Kulkarni said.

That's when Shrikant and Harleen came into their chamber where the IAT team was discussing the mission.

"Kulkarni, is your team ready for the mission?" asked Shrikant.

"Yes, they are ready."

"Great.Then the team will led by Harleen."

Harleensmiled and said, "Thank you, sir! I will be glad to lead the team! Is there any problem with you guys?"she asked, addressing the IAT team with a smile.

"Harleen, take your own decision and don't ask any second person about our mission.No one should come in between this!" said Shrikant.

"Okay, sir, I will," replied Harleen.

"Right, then get ready for the mission in France!" exclaimed Chief Shrikant.

After the meeting, all the agents involved in the mission gathered for some training with the arms and ammunitions and started to check them. Gaurav opened his drawer in the dressing room and took out his favourite Pistol Auto 9mm 1a. Right from the first day of his army career, this has been his favourite weapon.

On the day of their departure, they reached the airport on time. As Gaurav was boarding the flight, he got a call. It was from Indu.

"Hi Gaurav, where are you?" she asked.

Gaurav answered, "Hey, I am travelling abroad for some work, why, is this urgent?"

Indu replied, "No-no ... I thought of dinner tonight, so..."

"I think I will be out for 2–3 days. After my work gets done, I will call you and we will go for dinner."

When he hung up, Harleen asked, "Is that your girlfriend?"

Gaurav looked irritated and replied, "This is not about the mission, this is my personal life. So, if you think about the mission now, it will be good for us."

After 9 and a half hours of travelling in the plane, they finally touched the French Army Base.

France,

General Directorate for External Security,

As both the governments had agreed to work together to stop the next attack, the French authorities were already in the base to receive them.

As per the agreement, the FrenchauthorityhadappointedAgent Kane to help the Indian agents.Agent Kane and his team were already waiting for them when they landed on their base.They greeted and introduced themselves.

"Welcome to France! I am agent Kane from General Directorate for External Security. We are here to help you all."

Harleen said, "Thank you for agreeing to help us. I am Agent Harleen, leading this mission and this is my team."

"Is that it?" asked Kane confusedly.

Harleenreplied, "These are my fellow top agents."

On hearing this,Arushi and Gaurav and their team got angry with her behaviour.

Once they reached the base, Captain Iven, the head of the unit, came and told them, "On your authority's request,we are watching them.Till now there has been no movement and none of the groups havecome in or goneout.So, whatever help you need, we will provide you.But this is France; here we have our rules which you have to follow.So,watch and work."

"Okay,sir, we will," replied Agent Harleen.

"Agents, now onwards, agent Kane and his team will take charge. Kane, whatever information they want, give them," said Chief Iven.

"Okay chief," said Kane.

Harleen was about to say something when Gaurav took the lead and said, "Agent Kane, please give us the information about warehouse and everything you know about them."

Kanetook a look atHarleen's face as she was supposed to lead the team.

"Fine Kane, you may give him what he's asking for.He is our Analyst," said Harleen.

Then Kane handed the information to him,Danika and Gaurav also joined Varun.WhileHarleen and Arushi joined Kane for the surveillance.

Indian Embassy,

France,

As the prime minister of India had already entered the building and the meeting had already started, the agents didn't have much time to look around for the bomb.

After seeing all the information, they came to know that the address which was in the list this list belonged to a person who smuggled the weapons. Varun, Danika and Gaurav didn't get anytraceof their criminal activities orany criminal cases, so, Gaurav started to doubt whether they were terrorists or not.He went inform his fellow agents about his doubt.

"Agent Kane, are you sure that they are the terrorists?" asked Gaurav.

"Who are you?" asked Agent Kane.

"I am Gaurav,the analyst."

"I am sure.Our agents have kept an eye on them ever since the weapons were found and on tracking that location, we foundthat the address is registered to this warehouse," informed Kane.

"I think something is wrong," said Gaurav.

"What you mean?" asked Kane.

"I mean, they don't seem to be the terrorists," Gaurav replied.

"So, now you are telling me that we are wrong? Our agent tips can't be false.It is not similar to your desk job," scowled Agent Kane.

Kane got angry with what Gauravjustsaid. To fix things,Harleen quickly said, "Gaurav, I am in charge.First, you have to inform me, and then I get to decide!Don't make your own decisions!"

"I only said that they are not terrorists," Gaurav defended.

Harleen snapped back, "It has already been confirmed and they *are*terrorists.So, your work is over!"

Arushi stepped in, "Why you are acting like this?We are a team and we are supposed to support each other."

Harleen turned to her and replied, "You have to follow my order, that's all."

Arushi turned towards Gaurav and asked," What is it? Why do you feel that they are not terrorists?"

Varun joined the conversation, "After all the information we gathered, Danika and I traced all the activities but there are no suspicious activities there."

Gaurav said, "There is one more important information they didn't figure out—all the weapons and other things were transferred from the only one address."

"That means, without the knowledge of the house owner, the weapons were transferred to that address. So, high chances are that this is set up by someone."

Gaurav looked at Varun and asked, "Varun,can you track the weapons—where are they from by theirregistration numbers?"

"I will try," said Varun.

"What are you guys trying?First, we have to report to this to Harlean and Kane," said Arushi.

"There is no time for arguing.If my theory is correct, then those people in that house are in danger," said Gaurav.

Varun and Danika went to track the weapons.

Arushi called Harleen, "Harleen, please listen to Gaurav."

Harleenreplied with gritted teeth, "They are the Frenchintelligence!And they are perfect in their job!"

Arushipestered,"Can you please ask him to check for once?"

"We are on their land so they are helping us with authentic information.So, just trust them," replied Harleen.

"Can I see the file once again?"Arushi asked.

"Do whatever you want.They'll be calling in fiveminutes.After that, we are leaving, so be ready."

Arushi took the file and showed it to Gaurav, and said, "They are calling in five minutes.So, track fast!"

A minute later,Varun and Danika came and told, "Gaurav and Arushi, we've got the location where the weapons have been transferred to. And we think they are at the embassy."

"Ohno!How did I missthis?It had been theirplan!Thiswasa mere diversion!" cried Gaurav.

"We have to stop them!Send the force to the embassy immediately," exclaimed Arushi.

Arushi went to inform Harleen and Kane,but they were already trying to take the people in the warehouse,so, ArushicalledGauravand told him what they were doing. Gaurav then went to Harleen and Kane and tried to reason with them, explaining his observation, trying to make them understand the real plan behind all this.

"Kane, think about our clue. The target is the embassy!Try to think clearly," said Gaurav.

"But your team lead, Agent Harleen, has already gone to the warehouse to capture them," said Kane.

"No no! This is what they wanted!Arushi, please contact Harleen fast."

"Harleen, this is a trap, so, come back now!" cried Arushi over the phone.

"I have a clear target.I can't miss this," said Harleen.

"This is not about your ego.Please, for once, listen to us!Otherwise there will be innocents dying today," said Gaurav.

"I don't want to take any risk.I will go for it."Harleen was resolute.

Gaurav saw the warehouse through the binoculars and said, "Harleen, see through the thermal Camera."

But it was too late.She shot the bullet and a man fell dead.Gaurav shouted and asked her to see through the binoculars. When she saw, she found not a single dangerous man around. Both Harleenand Kane were in a state of shock. Arushi and Gaurav immediately came to rescue them but after the bomb was diffused from the man, all the people were taken out safely and the building got evacuated. But before they could run farther, they heard the bomb explode from the top floor. The people were safe, nobody got injured.

Gaurav commanded, "Kane, send the agents and the local authorities to the embassy fast, because the bomb is already implanted at the embassy!" said Gaurav.

"How did you know that?" asked Kane.

"This is not the time to answer, please send them; we have to go there!" said Gaurav.

After some seconds of reluctance,Kane sent the some of the agents to the embassywhileArushi, Harleen and Gaurav stayed back. Harleen, however, was still in shock from that shoot.

Arushi quickly took charge, "Kane,secure the area fast and find the bomb and try to diffuse it."

After further investigation, the bomb was finally found by some of their agents.

"But,Idon't understand..." said Gaurav.

"What happened?" asked Kane.

"This bomb is notasdestructive as I thought it would be. This can affect only a floor of this building," said Gaurav, perplexed.

He then showed it to Danika and Varun.

"Danika, how do we diffuse the bomb?" asked Gaurav.

Varun stepped in, "Show me the bomb."Varun looked at the bomb and started to diffuse it.

Finally they managed to diffuse the bomb but they failed to find any bomber or any terrorist.

After activating high alert, theterrorist escaped from the embassy. An hour later, a local traffic CCTV captured the man who had entered the embassy building with the box which had a weaponry brand label. After further investigation, they confirmed that he was the man they were looking for. After getting the footage of that, Varun shared the link with Gaurav.

Gaurav took a look at it and said, "Okay,then we have got our man so we have to capture him before he does anything else or even tries to escape the country."

"Right. We will keep an eye on him and every airport and alert all the law enforment Agency and transportation," said Kane.

"Thanks,Kane," said Arushi.

"No, thanks for helping in diffusing the bomb, and sorry for not listening to your information," said Kane.

"It's okay," said Arushi.

"Keep tracking him.If he sees you, immediately inform me or Arushi;

we are on our way to the embassy. And make the security tight," instructed Gaurav.

While they got busy to track the man, their eyes fell onHarleenwho was still in shock and stupor.

Gauravlooked at Arushi and said, "Arushi,go and talk to Harleen."

Arushi, a bit reluctant, asked, "Is this important?"

"Yes! We area team and if we have to complete the mission, we have to work together, please," Gaurav insisted.

"Okaythen."Arushi went to talktoHarleen.

"AgentHarleen, are you alright?"

"If Gaurav wasn't there, I would have ended up killingmore innocent people," trembled Harleen.

Arushiexplained, "In our work, this will happen. We have to control our feelings!"

"Thank god I had Gaurav and all of you, the entire team, or else I would have had to live with the burden of this all my life," Harleen broke down.

Arushi comforted her, "See, we are team ... if one of us makes a mistake, the other will have tofixit!Thisis what makes a team!"

"Sorry for being rude to you all," said Harleen.

"Well, if you feel sorry, then you have to help us catching the man who planted the bomb at theembassy.So, come on, let's go!"

They both resolved their differences and buckled up to crack this mission with a newfound resolution and team spirit.

Chapter 6
CHASING THE MAN

France,

General Directorate for External Security Base

After the attacked was stopped at Embassy, Gaurav ordered the French agents to check the CCTV for any suspicious man with any bags as per the order France authority agreed to check CCTV footage after a while of watching the CCTV they found a man who fixed the bomb at embassy after that immediately they informed to Agent Kane,

"Agent Kane, we have found the man who had planted the bomb at the embassy," informed the security head.

Kane said, "Okay, that's great then, send the CCTV footage to me immediately."

After receiving the footage, Kane showed it toHarleen and others agents.Watching that footage,Arushiasked, "Agent Kane, can you look him up in your criminal or terrorist records?"

"Of course I can!" said Kane and then he ordered his hacker to track that man.After sometime, their technician, with the help of face-recognition software, matched the person who was responsible for some terrorist activities throughout the world and was also among world's most wanted terrorists.This was informed to the agents. Seeingthese records, Gaurav got a clue about who was behind all of this.

Gaurav spoke up, "Ibrahim Syed, is a relative of the Mohammad Syed and I think there is a bigger problem in France until we find him."

"What are you saying?" asked Kane confusedly.

"I have been tracking him for almost a year but unfortunately could never find him.But this time I will not miss once again," said Gaurav, clenching his fists.

"So, what do we have to do now?" asked Arushi.

"Once he is arrested by the French authority, if we somehow manage to find who had come to visit him, then it is easy to track him ",

"Varun and Danika, you both contactKane and extract the information about him or know who visits him," ordered Arushi.

Varun and Danika nodded.

"You have to be fast because if we lose him this time, then there is no next time for us or for him.So, Kane,please make them incognito," said Gaurav.

"Sure we will," said Kane.

Iran,Tehran

After the unsuccessful attack on the Indian Embassy inParis, an informant of a terrorist group was contacted by Ibrahim, who informed him aboutthe failed attack.Then one of the men immediately went to meet Mohammad to brief him all about the attack.

Informant:Captain, the attack at the Indian Embassy has failed and the French authority has declaredahighalert all through the country.

Mohammad:Okay. Has Ibrahim contacted you?

Informant:Yes, after the attack failed, he contacted me.

Mohammad:Right, tell him about Plan B.

Informant:Okay captain.

Then informant then contacted Ibrahim butcouldn'tget through him even after several attempts.

Informant:Captain, his cell isn't connecting.

Mohammad:Keep trying.

Informant:I tried, but no use.

After listening to this, Mohammad got nervous and a bit tensed.

Informant: I think Ibrahim is in some kind of danger, don't you think?

Mohammad:If he gets into trouble, he will contact me but until now he hasn't.

Informant:So, what now?

Mohammad: Wait for some time, then we will think about it.

France,

General Directorate for External Security, Base

After sometime, the French authorities finally found out who visited Ibrahim in the jail.

Kane addressed the whole team, "Guys, we have got the list of everyone who had visited him in the jail."

"Who are they?" asked Harleen.

"Take a guess," said Kane.

Gaurav said, "I think Mohammad."

After checking the CCTV at the prisonand after sourcing valuable information from secret networks, Gaurav finally came to know that the man who had visited Ibrahim was none other than Mohammad.

"Yeah, that's true, Mohammad visited him in jail for five times during his stay there," said Kane.

"So, we know that he is linked to our mission, and he is linked to Mohammad.What about any of his friends or any relatives?" asked Arushi.

Danika smiled and said,"Right, he has a relative here."

Kane was surprised, "What?Relative?We didn't find anything about this!"

Danika replied, "We dug deeper and got the information."

"Who is that?" asked Harleen.

Gaurav interrupted, "Um ...I don't think it's a relative."

Danika said, "Correct.He isn't a relative exactly, but he was the landlord ofthe house Mohammad stayed in when he was in France. It seems like they got close and he helped this man a lot during the stay."

"Okay, then come on, let's getthis relative anddon'talert the public yet.If they come to know this now, they will get afraid and we may lose Ibrahim,' said Kane.

Gaurav said, "I do think that is a great idea."

"We have to catch him secretly, without letting out any information," reasoned Kane.

"Even if we raise alert, there might be danger for the people inside that house," Gaurav pointed out.

"So, what do you want to do?" asked Kane.

"Gather your agents.We shall silently get into that house because that man has got children as hostages!" informed Gaurav.

"Okay then, within a second we will be ready," said Kane.

Soon the team reached the house and stood outside for surveillance.

Kane said, "Guys, wait here; I will go insideandupdate you about that."

Arushi said, "Wait!Harleen, go with him."

"Me? I don't think so," said Harleen reluctantly.

Kane and Harleen went inside the apartment. Arushi asked through the ear chip, "Have you guysset your eyes on him yet or not?"

Kane whispered, "No, we don't have eyes on him yet."

"Look closer!"

A minute passed when Arushi asked again,"Ishe there or not?"

Harleen's voice came back, "We have a hostage situation here, we have to deal with it very carefully."

"What?We have to do something," said Arushi.

"Okay then, Kane and I will go inside," said Harleen.

"No, don't make a stupid decision, wait for a second.Let me think," said Gaurav.

In some minutes, Kane suddenly said, "I am hearing something, voice maybe."

"How many?" asked Arushi.

Harleen replied, "I think one."

After sometime, they heard a loud noise of a glass breaking.

"What was that?" asked an alert Arushi.

"It is the sound of glass breaking," said Kane.

"Ohno!Go inside fast!He is escaping!" exclaimed Gaurav.

After going inside, Kane and Harleen saw that two children and a man were tied to the chair.Harleen untied them.While Kane didn't give up on Ibrahim and, instead, chased after him. He leaped off hurdles and dashed and ran, until he had his hands on Ibrahim, who was no match to Kane's speed and flexibility. Kane tried to lock Ibrahim in handcuffs but Ibrahim suddenly smashed a stoneon Kane's head.Disoriented, Kane fell down on the floor. He tried to hold on to Ibrahim,butit was too late. Ibrahim had already escaped from the house.

Harleenasked Kane, "Did you find him?"

Kane panted, "No, he hasescaped."

Harleen replied, "Okay, just inform the others."

KaneinformedArushi and Gaurav about the same to whichArushitold Gaurav, "Okay then, Gaurav, contact Varun and Danika and tell them to put a surveillance on him."

"We have to do it really fast otherwise he can't be found," said Gaurav.

Gaurav called Varun, "Varun, can you track him through facial recognition?"

"Okay, I will do my best," replied Varun.

Varun then contacted local technician base for a live feed of all the street of France so that he can be found.The French authority gave the order to use that. After 15 minutes of searchinghim,they finally found him at a street and Kane and Gaurav were immediately informed.

Base,

Using the tracking surveillance, they finally tracked Ibrahim.

Kane said, "We got him using the VIN number so we will see where he will go."

Arushiimmediately spoke up, "What?No, we have to follow him!"

"No, nobody will diein my country!" said Kane

Arushisaid, "We know that, but if we see what he is capable of doing, then we will realize that he can do anything",

Kane firmly said, "I can't allow to do this mission."

Gaurav said, "If you are thinking of that blast, then it is nothing. If we didn't follow him, then we wouldn't know what their plan was and whom he was going to meet, because you saw that in thatapartment, they were communicating through the private chatting website.If only we saw the message, then we would have known how big their plan is going to be."

"So, what's your plan?" asked Kane.

"You have Aerial surveillance."

"Sowhat?"

Gaurav replied, "If we track him through the aerial surveillance, you will be able to lock his GPS tracker so we can follow him and also know where he will go or whom he will meet.So, please, this time listen."

"Okay,Iwill agree, but if he disappears, then what?"

"I don't think that will happen because you will lock his location," answered Gaurav.

Arushi said, "Okay then, we have to go now. Gaurav and Harleen, go with Kane and I will go with the other agents!"

They got divided into two teams and started following him.

Iran,Tehran

After listening to the phone call of Madiha, Rana was nervous and wanted to talk to her about that.Mohamad and his children were playing cards in the room when Madihacamein.Mohammadsaid, "Come join us to play."

"No, I am not interested," said Madiha in a small voice.

Her son, Ali, said, "Ammi, come on let'splay!Abba is also here!"

Even Zoya joined him, "Come na, Ammi!"

Madihagot angry and said,"No, I have already said it!"

Mohammad grabbed her by her arm and took her inside the room,"Whatare you doing in front of the children?"

"You think for my anger children will get afraid of me?Then what about you?"

"Don't talk about me, it is different," said Mohammad.

"No, you have to talk about this. Our children are getting scared because of all your work but you do not care about us.You have to stop this!You're doing all of this in the nameAllah. This is not good, you have to stop!" wailed Madiha.

Mohammad got enraged and slapped her and stormed outside.

France

After locatingIbrahim,they started to follow him in a car.

Kane asked, "Is it necessary to follow him like this?"

"Yeah, we have to know what he is doing," said Gaurav.

"Have you beentracking him for many years?" asked Kane.

"I have been tracking this group for a long time now.They didn't have any name or information about them, but I think Mohammad Syed is not the mastermind behind all of this," said Gaurav.

"How do you know," asked Kane.

"Because Abdul Syed has two sons, but for the world, Mohammad is his onlyson.We don't know about the other son.I think he isthe mastermind," said Gaurav.

"How did you find him?" asked Kane.

"We didn't.He is still is aghost."

"Then what?"

"We alsohave to become a ghost like him—be invincible—only then we will find him, otherwise no."

"Wow!You know everything about him," gaped Harleen.

Gaurav replied, "I have been tracking Mohammad for a long time, so…"

"I don't think so," said Harleen.

Arushi's call interrupted their conversation.

"So, where is he now?" she asked.

"He is driving, we can see him.Where are you guys?" asked Harleen.

Arushi replied, "We are 2 km behind you.",

"Alright then," said Harleen.

Syria,

At Midnight,

ASIUunit was transmitting a highly dangerous and most-wanted terrorist to a high-security protection jail and it was led by Agent Diana.

Chief told Diana, "Diana, we are transporting this person who is highly intelligent in bomb-making and hacking, so be careful."

"Okaysir, I will make sure I transfer him safely," said Diana.

"We got to be really cautious because some of our intel confirmed that one of our systems were hacked to see the criminal records. AadroopKhan was the man who stole records, paying the hackers hefty sum," said the Chief.

"Can't we track who hacked into our services?" enquired Diana.

"Yes, our hackers are doing that, but they say it has more firewalls for protection so they are taking longer time to crack the information," informed the Chief.

Diana "So, is that why we are transporting him?"

"Correctly so. Hence, please monitor the sky."

"Okay sir."

After some time, they all got ready and AadroopKhan wastakeninside the vehicle with handcuffs on and blindfolded as well forprotection. They had 10 jeeps with highly modern technology GPS-tracker.They started the journey.

Aadroop spoke up, "So, I heard that someone hacked into your servers."

Diana replied, "Some asshole thinks that they are cunning but they don't realize until they get an enemy who is more cunning than them."

"You're so beautiful ... you know that?" said Adroop.

"Yeah some have told me about that," replied Diana.

"You're so aggressive ... it is too much to control..."

Diana cut him short, "Shut up!"

"But you guys don't have a brain at all,"Adroop continued.

"Now what has happened?" asked Diana, perturbed.

"Don't you know, if someone can crack a highly secured army intelligence, then they can also hack modern-technology vehicle?Hahaha!" he guffawed.

Within seconds, Diana looked up in the sky and saw choppers flying above them, dropping bombs on them one after another. Somehow, Diana and other agents kept Aadroop safe and protected. Then they heard the noise of choppers get closer, where 10 men with gunslooked out and started to fire at them—all but not Aadroop. Soon Diana realized that they were here for Aadroop. Sheimmediately began to fire back, however, by then, they had already gotten hold ofAadroop and he was taken into one of the choppers which flew really low.But Daiana didn't give up; she tried to grab a man while thatchopper was taking off. Somehow, she succeeded to pull a man who fell off.Before Diana could do much, the man died.

Next Morning

SFU unit bombarded Diana with questions about what had happened the previous night. The Chief said,"All of your agents were killed and Aadroop was taken!"

Diana said, "I tried, sir…"

"No, you didn't try enough," the Chief replied.

"What could I have done, sir?"

"You couldhave called for the backup, but you didn't!Until you are clear from the higher authority, your dismissed," declared the Chief.

"Sir, are you thinking I helped him to escape?" asked Diana incredulously.

"This is not my opinion but it is the from the higher authority. So,submit all your stuff for now. Until you are clear, you are no member of SFU."

Diana left the unit with guilt.It was because of herthatAadroophadescaped and she felt terrible for this.

France

As they were following Ibrahim, the car stopped at some point.

Kane said, "Okay, the car has stopped.So, we will go."

"Right!Then I will call for backup," said Gaurav and then he calledArushi and said,"Wehave our target ready, we want backup."

"Will be in a minute, don't worry," said Arushi.

Meanwhile, Ibrahim's car parked at the gas station.

Gaurav immediately saw his chance. He told the other two, "The car is here, so, Kane and Harleen, you both take the front and I will take back."

"But there is no backup!" exclaimed Kane.

Harleen also joined, "Let's wait for backup."

Gaurav looked impatient, "There is no time!So, please, can we move?"

Kane and Harleensensed this too and monitored the front while Gaurav took care of the back but,unfortunately, he went inside bathroom which wasnearthe store. Gaurav was the one who saw him; he yelled, "Ibrahim!Stay where you are," warned Gaurav.

Ibrahim, shocked by the voice, quickly grabbed a boy from inside the store and held him hostage. He then said aloud, "I don't know who you are orwhich country you are from, but you have to put that gun down otherwise the boy will die."

The police, meanwhile, came to the spot. Ibrahim got scared and tried to escape with the boy in his custody. Gaurav ran after them to stop him but the police thought he was guilty and shot Gaurav's leg. Thesound of the gun was heard by Kane and Harleen, whorushed to the spot.Gaurav, despite being shot,kept running behind Ibrahim.

Kane shouted at the police,"Officers, we are from SFU!We will handle this now and that was our man whom you shot!"

Gaurav chased Ibrahim as he shouted, "Stop now! I won't waste my time here, so please tell me where are the upcoming attacks?"

Gaurav caught hold of Ibrahim and pinned him to the ground, punched his face, clenched his jaws, to make him talk.

Ibrahim spat and said, "You really want to know?"

"Where are the attacks?" Gaurav asked again.

"You know they cannot stop these attacks.You all are going to die," Ibrahim smirked.

As Gaurav and Ibrahim weretalking,Harleen came from behind

and punched him with the gun on his back andneck.Ibrahim, caught unprepared,left the boy whom Gaurav pulled to his side. Harleenthen pinned him to the ground and handcuffed him.Ibrahim was then being transferred in the van to theirunit.

Kane said, "You have got the man, come on, let's go!"

Each of them got into the car and started to follow the van in which Ibrahim was. After travelling some distance, the van suddenly exploded in front of them. The man Ibrahim died in that explosion.

Chapter 7
THE LEAKED CHATS

After the incident in France, the RAW agents got nothing else but the chat of both Mohammad and Iqbal which was used by Ibrahim to chat with his uncle Mohammad and taking that as evidence they left France to return to India.

India,RAW Headquarter

As they received the evidence from the Ibrahim, Harleen called Chief Shrikant, whothen informed the RAW chief, and all were called for a meeting.

"Okay, Shrikant, what have you got?" asked the RAW Chief.

"Sir, we didn't get Ibrahim, but we have found an evidenceabout how he communicated with his uncle Mohammad,"informed Chief Shrikant.

Disappointed, the RAW Chief said, "What is the use of that?We didn't get Ibrahim."

"Sir, we will figure something out.But according to the Frenchforensic,inside Ibrahim's body was an explosive, so he killed himself.We will figure out how," explained Shrikant.

RAW Chief replied, "You should, because no time is left.And good work, Shrikant!"

Shrikant said, "Not me,sir.This is done by my agent Harleen.She was the one who found the evidence from Ibrahim."

"Good work,AgentHarleen.Keep doing such good work!"

As they praisedHarleen, Varun and Danika were upset and angry. Unable to control any further, Varun said, "Hey, I am out of this unit after the mission is completed!"

"We all did this work but the credit goes to her," added Danika.

Kulkarni interrupted, "See, guys, this is your unit.Please be patient!"

Danika replied, "But sir, that evidence was found by Gaurav, but she is taking credit!"

RAW Chief spoke up, "So, Kulkarni, how are your agents working with their new unit?Tell them to learn something, okay?"

Varun, Danika and Arushi got angryaboutwhat happened at themeeting.After the meeting got over, Shrikant ordered Harleen, "Harleen, analyse the evidence and get me something else from that.You have to be fast!"

Harleenwas still in shock and was embarrassed about what had happened in France as well as in the meeting room. She simply nodded and replied, "Okay, sir."

Iran,Tehran

A truck entered Mohammad's house and 7 to 10 people were captured inside.They all were from India.Theywere taken down and locked into a prison inside the house.

At night, while Mohammad was searching for something in his room, he found three passports of his wife and his children.He was in shock, because he saw the passport and got confused and doubted his wife.Burning with anger,heset each of those in fire.

After that he went to the meeting with some leaders.Madiha and her children came to the room to sleep.Before going to bed, she went to see if thepassportswere kept securely.But when she opened the box,shewas shocked to see that it had disappeared.So she got paranoid, wondering if her husband got to know about the passports.She searched all over but still couldn't find it. After some time, she came across a piece of paper which was lying on the floor, half burnt.She bent low to take a closer look and was shocked to see that it was one of the passports. A chill ran down her spine. He knew. Madiha kept thinking what would now happen to her and the children. She stayed awake all night.

While the meeting was taking place,six to seven trucks came in and from one of them, Bilal got out.

He said, "Brother, we all are ready as you asked us to be."

"Okay then, let's start the work!" said Mohammad.

Bilal said, "But Bhaijan, is Iqbal alright or not?He didn't contact us."

"Don't worry, he will be alright.He will contact me tomorrow and will meet you at the destination," said Mohammad.

"Okaythen.We will meet you at the destination point and we will have success this time for all of our brothers who have sacrificed for this war in the name of theAllah!"

India,New Delhi

Hospital

After the meeting was over, all four of them went to meet Abhiramat the hospital.

"How are you,Abhiram?How does it feel in the hospital? Are you enjoying your holiday?" joked Gaurav.

Abhiramsmiled,"Come here, one bed is empty for you, so we both can enjoy here."

Gaurav and everyone else laughed.

"How was the mission?" asked Abhiram.

Arushi's face became small as she said,"It didn't go well."

Abhiram asked, "Why didn't you stop the attack?"

Varun began to say, "We stopped but—"

Abhiramcut him, "But what?"

"We didn't get him," finished Danika.

"You did well, you have saved a child.You should be proud!"Abhiram tried to motivate them.

"But you know ... I could have controlledbefore shooting Ibrahim, but I didn't have a choice.I had to save that child!" said Gaurav.

Arushi said, "You did well.You did what your heart told you to do, so don't need to worry ... we will find some way."

"How is your new unit?" asked Abhiram.

"Man, I will quit this job if wekeep working with this unit in the future," said Varun.

"Why?"

Danika explained, "Only Harleen got all the credit.We all did a great job in France but only she was appreciated and our chief was blamed and embarrassed in front of everyone!"

"We are not here to take credit, we are here to protect the country. So,lethertakethe credit and we will do our job," said Gaurav.

"Yes! Don't think of her, we will do our job," said Arushi.

That's when Indu entered the cabin for her round check-up.

"HI guys!How was your trip?" asked Indu, beaming at everyone.

"Oh, it was great!" said Arushi.

"Great! Abhiram, let's go to the lab for the scan," said Indu.

Arushi looked at Abhiram and said,"Okaythen,Abhiram, we will meet you afterwards!We have a meeting now."

"Okay guys, carry on with your work," said Abhiram.

They all left the hospital but Gaurav stayed back for a minute. Induasked the nurse to take Abhiram to the scanning lab.Abhiram smiled at Gaurav as he left the two alone.

"Sorry, I was in a meeting when you called that day," said Gaurav.

"It's okay," replied Indu.

"So, can we have dinner tonight?" he asked.

"Yeah, I'd love to!"

"Right then, at 9:00PM tonight, at the same restaurant."

"Okay! I will be there,"Indu said.

Gaurav got a call from Varun and had to leave for the meeting. However, outside the room stood Sakshi, who had heard everything about their date.

As they both left the room, smiling at each other, Sakshi followed Indu angrily. She confronted her at the canteen.

"What do you think you are doing?" Sakshi snapped.

"What?"Indu was completely taken aback.

"You are dating someone I hate very much and you didn't even tell me about it!"

"Sowhat?He is your brother and I thought you will be happy.I thought of telling you afterwards when the time was right.So, what's the matter?"

"I hate him very much!Because of him my parents were separated. In fact,his own parents died because he is like a bad luck.So, I don't want my friend to follow that track.Please don't date him ... he doesn't deserve you!Ialsofeel uncomfortable around him ... so please leave him.As you are my best friend, I want you to be happy, that's all!" Sakshi went on.

Induhad to calm her down so she said, "I understand.ButI will think about it ... so, let's grab coffee now, okay?"

"Okay, come on."

Iran,Tehran

As Bilal left the place with heavy weapons to the destination point, Mohammad joined a meeting with some group leaders.

Madiha, meanwhile, quicklypacked all her things and took her children to leave. That's when Rana, who had heard her talk to the VISA office, entered the room.Seeing him all of a sudden, Madiha got scared. She hoped that he didn't suspect anything, or else her husband would get to know it all.

"Why are you here, Rana?" asked Madiha.

"What are you doing?Where do you think you are going?" asked Rana.

"I am just packing my things topay a visit to my hometown,"Madiha made up.

"I know everything, I heard you on the call the other day."

Madihagot nervous and even scared thinking about what he can do about this, so she began to beg to him,"Please, let us leave and don't inform to your people and to my husband..."

"Why are you doing this to your husband?He loves you all so much," enquired Rana.

Madihalooked down and replied, "I know he loves us all, but you have to understand about my children's future! How would turn out to be, growing up in this atmosphere?What if my son becomes like his father?I can't live to see that! I am doing this for my children's sake, not for me.You have to understand ... please ... you also have a daughter... think about her, what if they come to know about your activities?We don't want to be a part of all these things you all are doing in the name of Allah.Iam requesting you to please let us live!"

After hearing everything, Rana looked around, seeing if someone was there.Once he was confirmed that there was no one around, he whispered toMadiha, "Get the children and your luggage quickly. I will show you the way."

Madihacouldn't believe her ears. She gasped, "Thank you very much!"

They hurried out of the camp through a secret route and arrived right outside the camp when Rana gave her the key of his van said to her,"I am doing this for the children.Because of our work, one of my daughters had died.I don't want the same to happen to them, so, get out of the country as fast as you can!"

She started the engine andbegan to drive fast.Theengine's noise alertedone of the men who saw Mohammad's wife drive away with the children.At that time, Rana was in the house, so, the man went to informMohammad ofhis wife and children's escape.

India,New Delhi

As all units were busy finding clues on Mohammad's next plan, looking for further evidences of him. But after thorough searches, they got nothing. They all were worried about this.

Meanwhile, Kulkarni and all his four agents were gathered in a restaurant to discuss the mission.Even after two hours of discussion nothing came out of it. Suddenly, Gaurav got anidea.

"Chief, I've got an idea!" said Gaurav.

"How confident are you about this idea?" asked Kulkarni, getting straight to the point.

"I don't know ... but I think it can work"

Kulkarni pestered, "How sure can you be about this?"

"I am a bit sure,Chief."

"Okay then, I will call the RAWChief, informing about this and call for a meeting," said Chief Kulkarni.

Arushi obliged, "Okay sir, then we will meet there."

Then they all left along with Gauravfor the Bureau.After they left the place,Indu came to the restaurant as she and Gaurav had a dinner date planned already.She waited for Gaurav to come to the restaurant.

RAW Headquarter

After Kulkarni briefed the RAW Chief, he arranged for a meeting with the PM and all other units.

"Gaurav, I am your unit head.You have to inform me first, not others," said Chief Shrikant at the meeting.

RAW Chief said, "This isn't the time for such arguments. It is about the safety of our country, so can we start the meeting."

The prime minister arrived at the RAW headquarter.

He entered the room and said with a note of urgency, "Without delay, tell me the solution of this problem."

The RAW Chief directed towards Chief Kulkarni, who handed it over to Gaurav.

Gaurav began, "Sir, after capturing Ibrahim, we searched the house where he was hidden and there we found some cards and a mobile phone. Our analysts, Varun and Danika,unlocked a chat with a person called 'Bhai'.After seeing the conversation, we came to know that he was escaping France with the help of someone.He managed to escaped after the plan of bombing the French embassy had failed.Even though we tracked him, unfortunately Ibrahim died."

"So, what now?" the RAW Chief asked.

Gaurav replied, "Sir, according to the terrorist group, Ibrahim is alive. Butwe and France know that he is dead ... so, we can trap them and use their cell number."

The PM heard Gaurav and then said, "Are you sure about this?Because if something goes wrong, they will expose us."

Gaurav replied confidently, "Yes, sir, I am."

RAW Chief looked at Chief Kulkarni and asked, "Howsure are you of this Kulkarni?"

Kulkarni replied, "Sir, I think 5%."

"Hmm ... then, there will be a risk."

Chief Shrikant spoke up, "Sir, if it is a risk, we can't do that."

"But this is the last chance we have got, sir"

PM finally said, "Okay then, proceed."

After thePMaccepted their proposal, they started to chat with the person whom Ibrahim was chatting with before he was killed.

Gaurav started the conversation with 'Bhai'.

Gaurav:Bhai, I have escapedout of the France,just according to the plan.

Bhai:Okay brother. I will sendhelp.Send me the location.Where are you now?

After some minutes of panic and confusion, Gaurav asked his team to track the location where they had spotted Ibrahim.

Gaurav:Okay Bhai, I am sending the location.

Bhai:According to our plan, we will win over enemy.All our men are in India now, so, within a short time our mission will start and enemy will be in our hand. All of thishas been possible only for you, my nephew!

On hearing this, Gaurav and all others in the room were shocked and silent which was broken by another message from Bhai.

Bhai:Okay then, in the name ofAllah!

Gaurav:Bhaijaan, in the name of Allah!

Gaurav was very careful while constructing the same phrase but another message came in.

Bhai:You are not my nephew.

Gaurav:No, Bhai, I am your nephew.

Bhai:No you'renot.Who are you?

Gaurav:How did you know?

Bhai:In the name ofAllah is the password.He has to give the id, but you gave the same phrase.

Gaurav:Can we call you Mohammad?

Bhai:Is my man dead?

Gaurav:He is dead.

Then suddenly the cell was shutdown.Theyall were confused.

"What happened Gaurav?" the RAW Chief asked.

Gaurav replied, "He has come to know about us."

"Then, what's next?"

"One thing is cleared—the man behind this is Mohammad."

PM said, "So it is for sure that theirmenare already in India.Now we have to be fully cautious.I am putting the country on red alert. You better gear up for this mission!"

"Okay, sir!" the RAW Chief said loudly.

Then all the units were delegated roles for the mission to check all the area.If anyone or anything seemed suspicious, theywouldhave to act upon it or arrest them and interrogate them.

Restaurant,

After waiting for Gaurav for almost two hours,Indu gotupset and angry. She began to consider what Sakshi had told about him and how he is a bad luck. She immediately called him.

Gaurav took her call, "oh, sorry,Indu! I was in a meeting."

Indu replied, "It is 10 PM now!What meeting can you have now?"

"Wait, I will be there in 10 minutes."

"No, your sister was correct. You don't deserve to have family or love … if you are not interested, just tell me!"

"Indu … that's not…"

"From now onwards, we will not meet each other"

Then she disconnected the call, leaving Gaurav confused. He didn't understand what just happened.

Tehran

After the chat with Gaurav, Mohammad came to know that his nephew, Ibrahim, was dead.He got angry and said to his men,"We will takedown India within 24 hours, so be prepared."

Then he grabbed all the captured people in the room and made them unconsciousbystuffing their faces with cloth-soakedchlorform.

Chapter 8
LONE WOLF

Iran,Tehran

All the leaders of the terrorist group came to know about Mohammad's family running away from him. They all got scared and angry with Mohammad, fearingthat his wife would tell the world about them.

One of the leaders, who was an old member of their clan, said, "Mohammad, we all have faith in you, but you didn't do any good to us or our people."

"What's the matter?" asked Mohammad.

"Your wife and children have escaped from you," said the leader.

"I will handle it, and it's my personal problem."

"No, not now.This is all our problem.If your wife exposes us, we all are going to die and what about our mission?How do we answer our superiors?" asked the leader.

"Don't worry,I will take care of them," Mohammad replied.

"You have to!Because if not, we will take care..."

"No, I will take care."

Mohammad then called Rana and told him,"Rana, go and search for them.If you find them, bring them back."

"Okay Mohammad, I will bring them back to you," said Rana.

The leader, however, interrupted and said to Mohammad, "One of our men will go with your men."

"There is no need—"

"No!This is now our problem.If your wife doesn't come, then our men will kill your family.If you approve to this, then only we will proceed with the mission.Otherwise, we will give the mission to someone else."

Caught in the bog, Mohammad was forced to agree to the leader. But Rana couldn't believe how Mohammad agreed to this.After they all went inside, Mohammad went to Rana and told him,"If the men try to kill my family, you have to protect them."

"Don't worry, I will protectMadiha. Sheis like my daughter," said Rana.

Rana then left the camp along with the other man to search for Mohammad's family.

Somewhere in Iraq,

After escaping from the camp, they stopped somewhere near Iraq to get food but Madiha noticed that her photo was with some guys with guns who enquired the residents there about them.She got scared, took her children and left the placeimmediatelyin the car. But it was seen by the one of the leader'smen.He instantly informed the leader about Mohammad's wife and children.Her location was soon shared by the leader with all his men.

India,NewDelhi

Hospital

After Indu called and hung up on Gaurav, Gaurav went to meet Induto apologize.

"I am sorry,Indu. I was in a meeting, so, I didn't pick up the call," pleaded Gaurav.

Indusaidthrough gritted teeth, "Right from the beginning you didn't tell me about your job, and what meetings you have at night!You keep giving excuses..."

"No, please listen, once!"

"Your sister was right!You don't deserve the love and family",

"Please listen"

"No, it's over!You're not interested in me, so I don't want to move further.Please let's breakup," she finished and left her chamber for the operation theatre for a surgery. Heartbroken, Gaurav quietly left the hospital.

He went to his mother and sister's grave and stood there, thinking about what Sakshi had told Indu, what Indu thought about him and everything.Time flew as he stood there still for hours he didn't measure.

RAW Headquarters,

After the meeting got over at the Bureau, all the units were busy in tracking Mohammad and his men.

"Hey, Gaurav is not taking my calls," said Arushi.

"Yeah, it's strange! He isn't taking mine either," said Varun.

Kulkarni entered the room and asked, "What's going on?There's a mission we have to complete!Where is Gaurav?"

Arushi said, "Sir, we are trying to call him, but he is not taking our calls!"

"Why?What has happened?He must have been here right now! Our country is at risk and he is not even here!" said Chief Kulkarni angrily.

"Sir, I think he is depressed..." suggested Varun.

"Oh! I think I know where he is. I will bring him back. Meanwhile, you all keep an eye on tracking those terrorists," ordered Chief.

Kulkarni straightaway headed for the cemetery. As soon as he reached, he knew his guesswas correct. Gaurav was there indeed! He went near Gaurav who looked up at him in moist, bloodshot eyes.

"Gaurav, what are you doing?" asked Kulkarni politely.

"Chief,I just came here to meet my mother and sister."

"But why are you crying?"

"Oh ... this ...Chief, I have been thinking about them," Gaurav wiped his tears quickly.

"You once told me that my son was like an elder brother to you; that means I am like your father ...So, tell me how you feel!"

"I feel like killing myself," Gaurav broke down.

"What are you saying?"

"Soon after I was born, my family died and the one whomI love so much, like my own sister,she hates me ... a-and now my love has also left me! So why should I live?"

"You still have a mother and a sister who love you so much," said Kulkarni.

Gaurav looked at him in surprise, "What are you saying?"

"I know about Iraq. I am your father's friend.I know everything!You should live for them and you're a soldier who fights for the country. Forget everything—but the most thing now isyou country which needs you the most!This is a good enough reason for you to live."

Gaurav wiped his tears and pulled himself together, "YesChief, you're right.We have a mission to finish!"

"Our guys are tracking Mohammad's people, so don't worry."

"I don't think that will be useful," said Gaurav.

"Then what do we have to do?"

"I have a plan," said Gaurav.

On hearing Gaurav's plan, Kulkarni agrees to it and they head to the RAW base.

RAW Headquarter

After reaching,Kulkarniarrangedfor a meeting and called the PM as well.

"What is it,Kulkarni?" asked the RAW Chief.

"We haveanidea,Sir," replied Kulkarni.

"What is it?"

"We have to takedown Mohammad, otherwise we won't knowabout their plans."

"No, that will be a risk,"said the PM.

"Sir, it will not be," reasoned Gaurav.

"Yes, PM sir, for the safety of our country, we have to takedown the camp," the RAW Chief insisted.

"Fine, but there cannot be any mistake!If people come to know about this, we will be exposed.So, take them down secretly," the PM cautioned the team.

RAW Chief said, "Yes sir. Shrikant, prepare your team."

Shrikant replied, "Okay sir, we have to go by air."

Gaurav quickly said, "No, sir, that will be risky because there are civilians kept as hostages and, most importantly, the world's topmost scientist has been captured by Mohammad.If we takedown by air, we will lose themall,sir.So, we have to take them down by ground."

"Right. Okay then, Shrikant, that will be a risk.So, we will attack by ground. Prepare yourselves. The attack will happen at 2200 hours," declared the RAW Chief.

The team geared up for the ground attack.

Somewhere Near Mohammad's Camp,

As they got the location of Mohammad's wife and children, Rana and the leader's men set out to search for them.Meanwhile, the other men of the leader's group were all out there, looking for Mohammad's family. After several hours of extensive search, theyfinally got them and then they were then captured and draggedto the jail. Rana and the man were soon contacted by these menand were informed that Mohammad's family was in their custody. As soon as Rana heard this, he got nervous and started to rake his brain, trying to figure out how to save Madiha and the children from such a peril!Along with the leader's man, Rana reached the location where they were locked in. They were taken to the jail. On the way, the men informed Rana that it was a long way back home and since it was already late into the night, it would be wiser to wait till the morning before heading home with their hostages—Mohammad's family. They decided the get ample rest for the night before theimportant journey.

After some time, when all the people in the camp went to sleep,Rana woke up silently and crept out of his room and went to the place whereMadiha and the kids were captured.Seeing them, he began to sob because Madiha was beaten was very badly andthechildren were in a state of shock.They all were scared. Rana carefully stole the key from the guard and unlocked the room.Madiha woke up with a start and flinched, but calmed down when she saw it was Rana.

"Madiha, wake up!We have to get out of here," Rana hissed.

Overwhelmed on seeing him, she hugged him and began to cry.

Rana hushed her, "Shh … silent!We have to get out from here now."

"But how we are escaping this place?There are so many people surrounding us from all the sides!"

"Don't worry about that, I will take care.You wake up the children. Wehave to escape right now!"

Madihathen woke up her children silently, and they got ready to escape.Quietly, in the darkness of the night, they escaped the camp not knowing anything else.

2200 Hours,

Iran,Tehran

As Shrikant's team was ready to attack, they were waiting for the final permission.

"Sir we are ready to strike."

Shrikant replied, "Okay, wait for my signal."

RAW "ok, captain they approve us to make strike so go on",

As soon as they received the permission to strike, the team landed by helicopter on Mohammad's camp and immediately they were attacked by the Mohammad's men. Bullets stormed out of guns in rage, the sky turned grey while the soil turned red. After what seemed like hours of bloodshed,one of the teams finally managed toenter the place where the people were captured, while another team went after Mohammad.But, to their surprise, there was nobody in that camp.After long search for Mohammad and his coreteam, they got nothing. They immediately reported this to the RAW, and the RAW gave them order to leave the camp with all the hostages and destroy the entire camp.

After that, they rescued all the people in a helicopter, and flew towards India.The remaining team left only after destroying the entire camp.

India,RAW Headquarter

After the mission was over, they called for a final meeting,

"So guys, our people are safe but we didn't capture Mohammad," said the RAW Chief.

Shrikant replied, "Sir, at least we have brought our people back safely!"

"Yes, but our PM is very angry that we didn't capture Mohammad."

"But sir, the camp was empty.Some of Mohammad's men were there, but the camp had no evidence or clues about their mission!"

"That means they knew we were coming," said Gaurav.

"We don't know anything about that, but we must capture him immediately otherwise there will be a problem," said the RAW Chief.

Chief Kulkarni suddenly got a call from Arushi,"Sir, we have got a suspicious audio through an army channel."

Kulkarni replied, "Okay, then bring that in."

Arushi, Varun and Danika entered the room.

The RAW Chief asked, "What is it Kulkarni?"

"Sir,looks like we've got some information."

"Then play it!"

As they played the video, they saw two men talking.

Person1:Bhaijaan, we have reached our destination.

Person2:Yeahmetoo.

Person1: When do we have to carry out the festival?

Person2: The festival will have to be tomorrow.

Person1: Okay,bhaijaan, we will meet there.

After watching the video, Gaurav informed the rest that these two men were Mohammad and Bilal.

"Where did we receive the signal from?" asked the RAW Chief.

"Sir, we have received the signal from India–Pakistan border,I think near Kashmir," said Arushi.

"Okay, then according to the audio, we heard that their plan is tomorrow.So, all the units must know this," said the RAW Chief.

"Sir, we can't be sure," said Shrikant.

Gaurav interjected, "We have only one chance, sir, we have to take it!"

They all finally agreed and left for Kashmir.

India,Somewhere Near Kashmir

After landing in Kashmir, the local soldiers and the team of the RAW spread all over the valleyto search for Bilal and Mohammed and their base camp.

"Varun, can you track the second person's signal?" asked Gaurav.

Varun replied, "Yeah, I will.Give me some more time."

"There is no time left."

"Okay, I will."

"Danika,sendBilal's photo to all the soldiers," instructed Gaurav.

"Okay, Gaurav."

He further added, "Arushi and Harleen will be here to assist you and Varun."

Varun suddenly said, "Hey, I got the location of the second person!"

"Great!Then I will inform Shrikant and send their team," said Chief Kulkarni.

"No, Chief, if we send the team, they will escape again."

Shrikant said, "Sowhat?There is no chance!I will inform RAW,"andthen he contacted the RAW chief.

"Sir, we have got Mohammad's location."

"Okay then attack them and capture Mohammad.Where is the location?"

"Wait, sir. Varun, what is the location?"

"Sir ... I think it is showing Pakistan's side of the border."

Shrikant wassurprised,"What?"

"What happened Shrikant?" asked the RAW Chief.

Shrikant replied, "The location is in Pakistan's side of the border."

"What?Then there will be some problems.Wait for my call."

"Sir, what did the chief tell?" asked Gaurav.

"He told ustowait for his call."

"Sir, we are delaying.If we delay further, he will disappear."

"Who is the chief?" scowled Shrikant,"you have to wait for the call."

Gaurav got angry but kept quiet. After some minutes, Shrikant got a call from the RAW chief, and Kulkarni received the call.

 "Kulkarni, the PM has approved the mission and gave us the permission. Kindly proceed with the mission."

"Great sir!We all are ready; we were only waiting for your order," said Kulkarni.

"Good. Then proceed for the mission," said the RAW Chief.

Kulkarni briefed about this to Shrikant and all the otheragents, including the IAT agents.

Shrikant ordered, "Varun, track the location of Bilal as quick as possible."

Varun promptly replied, "I am on it, give me a minute, sir."

After that, Varun started to track the location of the hiding place of Bilal. Once they found it, Varun shared it with the team andthen Gaurav, Arushi,Harleen and the other team members went to the location where Bilal was hidden.As soon as they got the location of Bilal, all the agents began to prepare and ready their arms and suits. They got in the car and drove to the location where Bilalwas supposedly hiding. They reached shortly, within a few minutes.

Harleen, being aware of the man's capabilities, ordered her fellow agents to be careful because he was the most dangerous man. After they stopped their vehicles at some distance, to make sure the terrorist couldn't see them, everybody stepped out of the cars and quietly covered the whole area.

"Okay guys, we are at the location of the Bilal, so, be careful.He is a dangerous man and we want him alive.He is the key to all answers to our question, so, we need him alive!" roared Harleen.

The agents nodded in agreement.The location where he was hiding was ina mountain area where there was an unused building, almost like an old warehouse.Harleen ordered some of her agents to go behind that building while some of them were ordered to man both the sides.Harleen and the IAT Agents, including Gaurav, attacked from the front of the building. As they reached the entrance of the building, they tried to unlock the door, but it was locked from the inside. It took them a minute to successfully and quietly unlock the door. They crept in carefully, without making any sound to make sure the terrorists were not cautioned. One of them peered in to check if the way was clear, and then he signalled the rest to follow him inside.

As they moved inside, one of them could hear a strange sound—that of a bomb detonating—and before they could react, they heard a huge explosion at the back of the building. Immediately, Harleen tried to contact the agents who were supposed to cover the back, but couldn't connect. The worst thought comes to Harleen—were they all dead?

The team began to move ahead, looking for trails or people around, when, suddenly, a couple of terrorists attacked them from behind. The sound of constant gunfire echoed, confusing the agents about the source of the gunfire. They all got distracted by it. Taking the chance of their distraction, the terrorists who were hiding, came out and began to fire at them mercilessly. Caught off guard, the agents dived for protection. The terrorists didn't stop; they didn't give the agents any time to fire back and kept firing furiously. Braving the situation, some of the agents decided to risk and fire back, but soon they were mutilated by the bullets.

Harleen cried, "We have to do something!Otherwise, we may not only loseBilal, but also many of our men!"

On hearing this, Gaurav looked at Arushiandsignalled her to cover for him.Arushinodded. Gaurav loaded his gun, closed his eyes, and took a deep breath. The images of both his sisters, mother, Aishia, Anu and Srivastava flashed before him. He then breathed out and made a move. He started firing back. He also activated a smoke grenade and rolled it towards the terrorists. Soon, they began to cough as the smoke made it difficult for them to fire or even see things properly. Gaurav used this opportunity and signalled his agents to fire back right then. Meanwhile, he, along with two others, moved up the stairs in search of Bilal or anybody inside. He looked into the rooms to confirm. As he kept climbing the stairs, all of a sudden, a man appeared in front of him. Gaurav wasted no time to shoot him. He fell down on the floor after which Gaurav silently move forward.

There was a man hiding in one of the rooms, waiting for Gaurav to enter the room.AsGaurav entered the room,the man started to fire at him but Gaurav somehow dodged the bullet and hid behind the wall.Gaurav kept still and didn't try to block him or fire back.After a few seconds,thefiring stopped. Gaurav could hear the man pressing the trigger but he realized that the gun was empty. Gaurav wasted no time and leaped out, onto him, grabbed the man and fell on the floor. The man struggled to free himself, he grabbed Gaurav's neck and tried to strangle him but Gaurav instead grabbed his head and made him fall on the ground. Gaurav pinned him to the floor and punched him hard. The man got hold of a heavy object nearby and tried to thrash it on Gaurav's head. Gaurav ducked but the upper part of his eye got injured and he started to bleed.As Gaurav fell down on the floor, the man grabbedagun which was nearby, but unfortunately the gun was empty. Gaurav by then had already reachedfor his gun and shot the man. With his eyes and head bleeding and throbbing, Gaurav somehow got up, took the gun from the dead man's hands, reloaded it, and tucked it in his suit along with his own gun. As Gaurav proceeded, many men came his way but Gaurav kept shooting them dead one after another. After some more minutes, the team got together at one point.

Harleen asked, "Where is Bilal?Wecouldn't find him in this building."

"I think he is in this room," said Gaurav and pointed to one of the rooms.

As, everybody got ready to enter the room, all of a sudden, there was heavy firing from inside the room. Everybody took a shelter behind the pillar.A few seconds later, the door creaked open and then Gaurav took this opportunity. He signalled all his agents to attack at the same time.Then all the agents, including Gaurav himself,began firing furiously. Some of the men fled away inside the room. Gaurav got suspicious as his eyes searched forBilalwho was nowhere to be seen. Gaurav began to doubt if he was escaping from behind. He immediately calledArushi, who was standing near him.

"Arushi, cover me.Do you have some magazine?"

Arushi handed Gaurav a magazine with bullets loaded in it, and Gaurav walked towards them with no fear while firing at them. HarleenwatchedGuarav in awe, surprised by his courage and bravery.All the others agents covered him as he entered the room. When he entered, he saw that they had escaped from the building with a rope handing from the window to the ground. Gaurav peered through the window to look below and saw that Bilal and some other terroristswere escaping in a car. Just before getting into the car, Bilal looked up and began to fireat Gaurav. Caught by surprise, the bullet unfortunately hit Gaurv's hand and he immediately ducked below the window.The terrorists escaped.Arushi and Harleen and other agenst entered the room but before they could blink, Gaurav jumped out of the window.

Arushi screamed out his name, "GAURAV!"

But, bythen Gaurav had already jumped out of the building and

Harleen and Arushi dashedto the window to see what happened to Gaurav. They saw Gaurav get into a car and chase the Bilal's car. They too followed Gaurav immediately.

Gaurav accelerated his speed to capture him. After trying to chase him, he finally spotted Bilal's car.There were two cars, one is front and other one behind that car.As soon as Bilal spotted Gaurav chasing them in that narrow road, they began to rain bullets at Gaurav's car. Gaurav tried to dodge them by driving in a zig-zag manner.

NewDelhi,

In the meantime, Sakshi, who was on duty,receivedacourierat the hospital. One of the nurses handed her the parcel, seeing which Sakshi was surprised. "Who would be sending this?" she thought. There was no name on that parcel.She quickly opened it curiously. In that she found a dozen of letters, all written by Gaurav long time ago but were never posted or delivered.It also had some gifts like a watch, dolls, greeting cards and other gifts which he had tried to gift her on her birthdays and every year. However, they were all stored safely with Gaurav, who never mustered the courage to send them to Sakshi. Sakshi took out the topmost letter and began to read it.

Dear Sakshi,

I know you don't like me. I agree with you when you say that it was because of me that your parents got separated. I guess I deserved all this. But you know, I love you so much! I don't have anyone else in this world except you, mother and father. I know you don't look like me or consider me your family member, but you will always be my sister. I will do anything you want to keep you happy and safe along with mother and father. You know, every birthday of yours, I would buy a gift for you but I then, as anafterthought,Ithinkit's a bad idea. All these years, I have seenyour birthday celebrationfromafarand I too would celebrate your birthday. You must know thateven if you don't accept me as your family, I am okay with that, but you must remember that I will be your brother till my last breath and even after that if it's possible. If you're reading this letter, that means I will not bother you again.If this gives you happiness,I will not meet your family, so, please tell mother and father that I loved them very much and I am sorry for whatever I had done wrong with or without knowing. But you have to remember that I will always love you all. You all are the only family I have.

Love,

Gaurav

As Sakshi read the letter, she magically had a change of heart and immediately left the hospital.She drove back home.

Jammu And Kashmir,

Gaurav was chasing the car full of terrorists whowerefiring at Gaurav's car.Harleen and Arushiwerefollowing Gaurav. As they neared his car, they saw how the terrorists were targeting him. They immediately called Gaurav.

"Gaurav, what are you doing?" asked Arushi.

"He is our last hope, our last link to the blast and Mohammad. I can't let him escape," said Gaurav.

Harleenspoke up, "The army men are chasing him too, and they will capture him."

"You know I will not stop," replied Gaurav.

Just then, Gaurav's car collided with one of the terrorist's cars and they shot bullets at him. Harleen and Arushi went cold, wondering if Gaurav was alright.

 "Gaurav, Gaurav are you there?" they shouted at the speaker.

There was no response from Gaurav. But within seconds, they heard firing from Gaurav's car and then they heaved sighs of relief. After what seemed like hours of chasing and dodging bullets, Bilal's car hit a rough edge of the mountain and crashed, sparks flew out of the car. Gaurav stopped his car ran towards the car. It was about to catch fire so Gaurav quickly grabbed Bilal and pulled him out of the car. Meanwhile, Harleen and Arushi arrived on spot, followed by the other agents. Bilal was bleeding profusely. Gaurav held him by his collar and punched his face with bleeding hands.

"Where are the attacks?" Gaurav growled.

"You are too late.Bhaijaan's plan will work and all you Indians will suffer for that," smirked Bilal and almost immediatelyhe pointed a gun at himself and shot himself.Unfortunately, they couldn't get any information about the attack.They kept searching the room frantically where Bilal and his men stayed.After hours of frantic search, at one point, they got some information about the attacks.

Gaurav immediately called Varun, asking him to crack the

code,"Varun, I am sending you a code.Crack it now!"

"Right, send me!"

After a while, Varun called, "It is the location where attacks will happen."

"Where are those places?"

Danika's voice came in through the phone, "Delhi, Mumbai, Bangalore, ChennaiandKashmir."

"Inform the RAW Chief to disarm the bombs immediately, and send me the location of the bomb inKashmir!"

Varun shared the location with Gaurav but just before disconnecting the call he said, "Wait! The secondperson'slocation and the place of attack seems to be the same! And there will be problem"

"What?Are you saying?" asked Gaurav.

"The location where Mohammad is hiding is the market place it is very crowded,"informed Varun.

"Are you sure about that?" asked Gaurav.

"I am sure!"

Gaurav turned to Shrikant and said, "Sir, Mohammad will attack that place, we need to capture him before that, otherwise, he will succeed."

Shrikant replied, "Okay.Then we will arrest Bilal and we will be in the camp and Kulkarni capture Mohammad and return to base camp."

Before anyone could register what is happening, Bilal seized a gun from one of the agents and shot himself in the head. He was dead on spot.

Kulkarni and other agents had no time to waste as theygot into the car and drove straightto the location ofMohammad.As they reached the location, they realized how difficult it would be to track Mohammad here. It was an extremely crowded place.Gaurav took the mobile and started to track the location sent by Varun.

Kulkarni said, "Guys, be careful!There are innocent people around; don't shoot.We want Mohammad alive, so we have to do it as silently as possible."

They all nodded, loaded their guns and dispersed, in search of Mohammad.

As it was a crowded market, the agents were unable to see any of those targeted faces.Some of the agents were being fired at from behind and they dropped dead. Kulkarni tried to contact them but there was no response.In the chaos and clutter, the men from the terror group silently reached the agents from behind and twisted their neck in a gesture that killed them on spot.

"Agents, they knew that we are here so, be careful. I think some of our agents are taken down," said Kulkarni.

As per Kulkarni's order, every agentattentivelybeganlooking. He further added,"If anybody sees anything or anyone suspicious, take them and search them. If they are proven to be terrorists, then silently get rid of them. Andif anybody looks even remotely suspicious, then corner them and get them to me."

As Arushi and Harleen looked out for suspicious activities, two men came from behind and tried to take them down, however, the girls were fully prepared. They quickly shot them with their silencer guns and took them down instead, making sure that no one in the marketplace could make out this fiasco.

Gaurav walked silently into the market and moved forward when a man walked from the opposite direction. Gaurav din'tpay much attention to him but as he came nearer, Gaurav noticed that he hadhad a knife and agun in his hand. Before the man could stab or shoot,Gaurav grabbed his arm and pushed him behind the shop, away from the notice of the crowd. But in a quick move, the man managed to pierce the knife into Gaurav's stomach. Air left Gaurav's lungs as he writhed in pain. The man took the knife out and attempted to stab Gaurav once again but Gaurav didn't spare another chance. He took him by his arms and twisted it until he heard a bone snap. Then he went for the neck.The man collapsed on the floor, lying still. Gaurav then removed the body to a corner, took the gun which had fallendown on the floor and checked if it was functional. Gaurav then continued to move forward silently. After covering some distance, the tracker finally starts blinking, indicating that the location of the Mohammad was nearby.All the agents gathered at that same point—near an old building of three storeys made of wood.

Kulkarni calledShrikant, "Shrikant, we are at the location and we are taking him down."

Shrikant replied, "Okay, aftercapturing him, comes to the base."

Kulkarni agreed and ordered all his agents, "We want him alive!Be careful!"

Agents agreed to that and Kulakrni divided them into three teams: one was supposed to attack them from the back of the building and second team from the front of the building, while the third team would attack from the side of the building. as per the senior officer order all agents agrees move to their location and as the back of the building Harleen and Arushi and some of the agents move towards the back of the building Kulkarni and Gaurav and some agents from front of the building and third team by side of the building, as they move forward they didn't see anyone in building as it is silent but in a second some where from the market bomb get explode and people in the market get scared and start to run in fear and screaming for help as terrorist made this to distract the Indian agents to shoot at them the agents gets cover from the pillar of the buiding, shop and vehicles. Gaurav didn't see bullets where it is coming from as the crowd in the market are running to save there lives but in that crowd and young girl who fell down on the ground while running with his mother but the mother didn't get notice about that as there's crowd she runs as she thinks that she is holding her daughter hand, and that is seen by Gaurav and then suddenly women comes to know that her daughter is not with her and start to look for her as she sees her daughter she start to run towards her, and then Gaurav sees a man shooting the gun at the same direction where the wo man is running to protect her daughter as the Gaurav sees that and takes out his gun and run towards her while firing at them and grabs women and her daughter and hide behind the big vehicles, as they rescues them women thanks him and woman grabs her daughter in arm and runs far away from that place. As Gaurav sees that be heard the chopper sound and he thinks that Mohammad is escaping so, Gaurav signals to Kulkarni about the chopper and asks Kulkarni for his another and Magzine and Kulkarni gives them all and asks Kulkarni to cover him as he stand up start to shoot at the terrorist and move forward very quickly as possible to enter the building and he breaks the door and successfully enters the building. As Gaurav enters the building as he sees no one inside the building as he enters the building other agents and Kulkarni enters the building behind him.And then Kulkarni signals to his agent to search the terrorist and take down them. And they scattered in the building in search for the terrorist.

And then Gaurav look for the Mohammad but instead Mohammad subordinates are blocking the way so Gaurav gets angry and reloaded his gun and move forward to them in bravely without hesitation and start to firing the gun at them and Gaurav reaches back of the building but then Harleen and Arushi comes to that point ,

Gaurav "you didn't found Mohammad?,"

Arushi "no, we didn't found him on our way here,"

But, then they hears the chopper blades rotating sound from the distance of them and then Gaurav turns to that direction and Gaurav sees Mohammad who ruuning towards teh chopper with his three subordinates to enter into helicopter, as Gaurav sees that he start to run towards the chopper to stop him but Mohammad know it already that they are coming so setup a land mines and as Gaurav start to run towards the chopper the land mines get activated and starts to explode but the Gaurav didn't hesitate to that as he runs towards him as if there is no explosion is going on there, Mohammad sees that order his subordinates to shoot at Gaurav and as they did Gaurav fire back at them and then Mohammad enters the chopper order his one of the subordinates to stay and shoot at him but, Gaurav shoot at him and one of the subordinates of the Mohammad fell down on the ground as he reaches the chopper the chopper already flew some distance from the ground, as Gauarav sees that he sees big truck standing there and Gaurav runs to that climbs the truck and jumps to catch the chopper and Gaurav successfully did and grabs the helicopter. As all agents and Kulkarni are seeing this they try cover Gaurav from the other terrorist who are firing at Gaurav.

As Gaurav successfully climbs the chopper one of the subordinates try to kick Gaurav's hand and he did several times and but Gaurav escapes that and last Gaurav takes out his gun and fired at him and subordinates fell from the chopper. And Gaurav reaches inside the chopper but then other subordinate try to fire at him but instead Gaurav shoot at him, and he fell from the chopper. And Gaurav enters the chopper as he enters the chopper Mohammad trys to takes a shoot at him but Gaurav punch to his hand and gun fell down to the ground and Mohammad punches to his stomach where he is having pain and Gaurav fell to the sit in painand try to garbs his neck but Gaurav instead grabs his neck and makes Mohammad calm and try to chat with him,

Gaurav said, "So, tell me what is your plan."

Mohamad "You think that you've won, but you are wrong",

"What does that mean?" asked Gaurav.

"You think that I was the mastermInd behind all of this, but you're wrong."

"What?Tell me about the mission!"

"First you have to promise me..."

"What?"

"You have to protect my family…" Mohammad took out his wallet and showed Gaurav the picture of his wife and children.

"Okay, I will protect. But first tell me who is behind all this?"

"Your country has an insider, who is giving all the information abouteachofyour steps and plans…"

"Give me the name!"

"I don't know …but if you think this was the original plan, then you are wrong.Thiswas only a distraction. The original plan will come soon … wait for it…" Mohammad heaved a sigh and died. This was followed by a massive explosion. Varun, But, then Pilot of the chopper trys to kill Mohammad then Gaurav rescues Mohammad in the action Gaurav fires at the pilot and chopper gets machine fail and goes down to the ground in the matter of few seconds the chopper fell on the mountain as all agents are seeing that they get shocked that chopper gets blast in which Gaurav present in that chopper. And in that blast Mohammad and Gaurav get killed.

NewDelhi,RAW Headquarter

After the mission all agents reached New Delhi and submitted all the equipment which wereseized from Bilal's place and produced them infornt of the RAW chief.

"Mission was successful but we lost so many of our agents and our Analyst Gaurav.This success is dedicated to them and Gaurav," said the RAW Chief.

"Sir, we need to give them an honourable funeral," said Kulkarni.

"I agree with you and but you also know that RAW agents can't expose their names, but I will still talk to PM and arrange for that," said RAW Chief.

As IAT agents—Arushi, Varun, Danika and Harleen—they all were in pain of losing Guarav.

And then they reached the hospital where the Abhiram was admitted.

On seeing their pale faces, Abhiramenquired, "What happened?Was the mission successful?"

Arushireplied, "Yes, mission was successful."

Right then,Indu entered the room and then Varun turned the TV on. He put it on a news channel. Soon news flashed regarding the success of their mission, followed by the deaths of their martyred soldiers. Abhiram looked at his team in helplessness and disbelief; Arushi silently gestured, as if validating the news. Indu, who had no idea who Gaurav was in real, innocently looked at the headlines and said, "Unsung heroes who gave their life to the nation for the victory."

Nobody had the heart to break the news to Indu. They gulped the bitter sorrow and remained numb.

Srivastav's House

Just when Sakshi and Srivastava were discussing the letter written by Gaurav, they heard the news. The mission was a success. But India lost some of her men. Gaurav was one of them; he was no more. Shock followed by silence took over the Srivastava household.

Before they could register the news in their minds, Kulkarni arrived at their threshold.

Srivastav saw him and marched out, "Kulkarni! What is this? Is this true? Gaurav is dead?"

Kulakrni paused a bit and said, "Yes, what you're hearing is true.He is dead."

Srivastava shook his head rigorously. "No ... he can't be dead ... he told me that he will be back!"

"We saw with our own eyes, Srivastava, he is dead," said Kulkarni and then handed a box to Sakshi and her mother.

"What is this?" asked Anu.

"It's from the Gaurav's locker which is written inyour and your daughter's name," replied Kulkarni.

Anu opened the box and in that she found some gifts, a letter and some other things. Anu opened the letter and began reading.

"Dear Mom,

I know you don't like me calling you mom but you know,right from my childhood you are my mom. As much you hate me, I love you. I don't have words to express my love towards you. But, one thing, whatever you think of me, I will always be your son and youmy mother."

Anu began to open the gifts and then broke down.Tears trickled down her cheeks as she remembered all those moments she had ill treated this son of hers.

And then Sakshi opened her box and bank papers which claimed that all the money that Gaurav had in his savings account would now be inherited by his sister, Sakshi.

Kulkarni walked towards a grieving Srivastava and handed him a watch.

"What is this?" Srivastava asked.

"Gaurav wanted to give this to you as afinal gift."

Shattered, Srivastava quavered bleakly,"What about their funreal?"

Kulkarni sighed, "You know the rules of RAW … we can't expose the name of our agents, so there will be funreal for all of the agents including Gaurav, but secretly."

Sakshi looked up in surprise and asked, "What?Dad! Gaurav was also a RAW agent?"

Srivastava broke down.

Before leaving, Kulkarni asked the family to reach early on the day of funeral as family had to be there. But Srivastava cried, "We are not his family!"

"What are you saying dad?We hated him so much but instead he loved us all … we have to pay him respect. That's the least we can do now!" said Sakshi.

"I didn't mean that. Gaurav has a family," said Srivastava.

"What! What are you saying?" asked Anu incredulously.

"Yes, he has a family."

"What? Family? Where are they?" Kulkarni too was surprised by this new and shocking revealation.

"They are in Syria."

"Then call them and ask them to come to India for thefunreal," said Kulkarni.

After Kulkarni left, Srivastava slowly took the phone dialled upAishia's number.

A voice greeted from the other side. "Hello!Who is this?"

"It's me, Srivastava," he said in a low voice.

"Hello, Srivastav, how are you?"

"I am fine,how is your daughter?"

"She too is fine."

"Gaurav told me everything about you all..."

"But Diana doesn't know about all this at all!What about my son? How is Gaurav?"

Srivastav paused a bit and finally said, "I called because of that."

"Why? What has happened? Is Gaurav alright?"

"No ...we ... we lost him in a mission..." Srivastava's voice broke down.

"What! NO! It can't be..."

"He went for a mission but that took his life ... I am sorry."

Aishia was in complete denial as she said, "NO!He had promised me that he will come to see me and his sister!"

"We have to accept it, Aishia. Please come to India with Diana and pay your final respect to your son."

Once the call was disconnected, Diana, who was hearing her mother all this while, said, "You're talking about some brother—what is that about?"

Aishia simply stated, "We have to go to India urgently,right now!"

"You have to tell me now," insisted Diana.

Aishiareplied, "Trust me, I will tell you everything when we land in India."

They both packed and got on the next available flight to India without another word.

New Delhi,

The flight that brought Aishia and Diana to India also had someone else onboard. It was none other than Aadroop Khan. Diana was waiting at the immigration when her eyes caught a sight of him. He stood quite far away to be certain about his identity. Just as Diana was trying to get a closer look, her name was called out and her mother pushed her to walk ahead. The mother and the daughter stepped out of the airport to see Srivastava already waiting outside to receive them.

Srivastav looked at them and then said, "I thought you will not come."

"How can't I? My son has died! I have to attend his funreal!"Aishia broke down, finally.

"What? Whom are you talking about?" asked a very confused Diana.

Aishialooked at her daughter and said, "You will understand everything in a short while."

Srivastava drove them to the RAW Headquarters where, on reaching, they saw that Srivastava's family was already there; and sowereArushi, Varun, Danika, Abhiramand, surprisingly,even Chief Kulkarni. Kulkarni came closer to receive them and then took them to his chamber.

He offered them some water and then slowly said, "Madam, we are extremely sorry for your loss.Both, your husband andyour son,sacrifiedfor our country..." Kulkarni trailed off and then handed them a box full of Gaurav's photos and belongings.

Seeing them, Diana shrieked,"Mom! What is that?What has happened to Gaurav?"

Looking down, Aishia slowly replied, "Gaurav is your brother..."

The news crystallized the air around as Diana felt the air sucked out of her lungs. She was numb with shock and pain.The funeral began. It was a private affair, humble enough to not grab much attention as the world can't know about Gaurav.Once the funeral was over, one by one, people started to leave—all except Gaurav's team mates and family.

Diana went on to open the box that was handed to her. It had a beautiful handwritten letter from Gaurav. She began to read it.

Dear Mom and Sister,

I didn't get the chance to meet you guys for all of these years … and Iwould always think I'm alone and felt miserable about that. But when I met you both, my happiness knew no bounds! I felt very happy that I got my family back.All I want now is my Mom and sister to be happy—with or without me. Daina, I am sorry I didn't tell you that I am your brother. I genuinely want both my sisters to be happy. Once agin, I am sorry if I have disappointed you all.

Love,

Your brother, Gaurav.

As Daina read the letter, she looked at the grave of Gaurav and said in a trembling voice, "Brother, I love you and will always do till the end of my life," and thenshe hugged her mother and broke down. All the agents, includingArushi, Varun, Danika, Abhiram and Harleen recalled all the memories they sharedwith Gaurav as they saluted and paid their final respect to his grave.

Aishia, while consoling her daughter, suddenly caught attention of a black Mercedes car right outside the cremation ground. A man sat inside, watching them all from there. Overcome by suspicion, as soon as Aishia peered to get a better look, the man rolled up the glasses and drove away.

The man in the car was none but Aadroop Khan.

After the funreal got over, Aishia and Dainaleft for the airport to catch a flight to Syria.

Somewhere Near Iran,

While Madiha was fleeing with her children in a bus, she overheard some men talk about the death of the most dreaded man— Mohammad. Unable to control her emotions, Madiha immediately asked the bus driver to turn on the news on the bus's TV. The news was confirmed; her husband was dead. Mixed emotions engulfed Madiha. While she lost her husband, she knew deep down that at least her children will grow up in a better environment now, that she will be able to give them a healthy life now.

Meanwhile, in Delhi, all the information and data about Gaurav was erased. He was no more regarded as a part of the RAW and all the information that was attached to him were transferred to a secured and locked file categorized as 'Confidential'. The news that was flashed all over media was that the most wanted terrorist, Mohammad, was dead in an explosion during the mission, but the media didn't get any information about Gaurav. Gaurav became a mere casualty—an unknown man who accidentally died in that explosion.

After a Week,

Varun and Danika were tracking a person but then suddenly they got an alert in their system. They immediately opened to see what was this about. What they saw left them perplexed—someone had hacked into their system, trying to access a classified file of an Agent. They immediately informed this to theRAW Chief.

"What are you saying?How could someone hack our system? It's fully encrypted and secured!" exclaimed the Chief.

"Yes, sir, someone has hacked a classified file of one of our agents," said Kulkarni.

"Whose classified file was that?" the Chief asked.

"Sir, of an ATU agent, Arjun, who was dismissed from the Agency," informed Kulkarni.

"Do you have any idea how grave this is? Where is Shrikanth?"

"Sir, he is on a mission."

"Alright. Then you lead the team and solve this as soon as possible."

"My team is already tracking the hacker, sir."

"And give me all the details of this Arjun. I want to know everything about him."

Chief Kulkarni and his entire team got worked up and split into two—one group scanned through every file to extract as much information about Agent Arjun as possible, while the other group, the cyber experts, invested hours to track this hacker who dared to breach RAW files.

Someone out there smirked in delight.

www.ingramcontent.com/pod-product-compliance
Lightning Source LLC
Chambersburg PA
CBHW021959120726
47992CB00001B/335